One for the road . . .

Joe didn't realize it, but he was quite an apparition to be-hold. He stood there, just inside the swinging bat-wing doors, ashen-faced, holding his hand over a wound which spilled bright red blood between his fingers. He surveyed the room for just a moment, then, with great effort, walked to the bar.

"Whiskey," he ordered.

The solemn-faced bartender poured him a glass and Joe took it, then turned around to face the silent patrons. By now his side was drenched with blood from his wound, and the blood was beginning to soak into the wide planks of the floor.

"Joe!" Alice said, moving to him quickly. Joe held his hand out to keep her away.

"If any of you had anything to do with me getting knifed, I'm going to give you fair warning. The next man who even looks at me cross-eyed, I'm going to pull him apart with my bare hands." Joe looked at them, tossed down the drink, then set the empty glass on the bar. After that, he walked calmly from the bar. . . .

BUSHWHACKERS

HANGMAN'S DROP

B. J. Lanagan

JOVE BOOKS, NEW YORK

This is a work of fiction. Names, characters, places, and incidents are
either the product of the author's imagination or are used fictitiously,
and any resemblance to actual persons, living or dead, business
establishments, events or locales is entirely coincidental.

HANGMAN'S DROP

A Jove Book / published by arrangement with
the author

PRINTING HISTORY
Jove edition / January 2000

All rights reserved.
Copyright © 2000 by Penguin Putnam Inc.
This book may not be reproduced in whole or in part,
by mimeograph or any other means, without permission.
For information address: The Berkley Publishing Group,
a division of Penguin Putnam Inc.,
375 Hudson Street, New York, New York 10014.

The Penguin Putnam Inc. World Wide Web site address is
http://www.penguinputnam.com

ISBN: 0-515-12731-0

A JOVE BOOK®
Jove Books are published by The Berkley Publishing Group,
a division of Penguin Putnam Inc.,
375 Hudson Street, New York, New York 10014.
JOVE and the "J" design
are trademarks belonging to Penguin Putnam Inc.

PRINTED IN THE UNITED STATES OF AMERICA

10 9 8 7 6 5 4 3 2 1

BUSHWHACKERS

HANGMAN'S DROP

Chapter 1

THE SHOCK WAVES OF THE EXPLOSION MOVED ACROSS *the field and hit Win Coulter, making his stomach shake. The blasts were set off by long fuses, but were timed to go together, starting as bursts of white-hot flame, causing black smoke to erupt from under the points where the charges were laid. The underpinnings of the trestle were carried away by the torpedoes, but the superstructure remained intact for several more seconds, stretching across the creek with no visible means of support, as if defying the laws of gravity. Then, slowly, the tracks began to sag and the ties started snapping, popping with a series of loud reports like pistol shots, until finally, with a resounding crash and a splash of water, the whole bridge collapsed into the creek.*

"Now, that's the way to do it, boys," Quantrill said exultantly. "We dropped her into the water just as neat as a pin!"

"The Yankees won't be movin' troops over this railroad for a while," Joe Coulter said.

"I suppose not," Win replied.

"What's wrong, Big Brother?" Joe asked. "You don't

sound very pleased about it. It was a good job, and it'll deny the Yankees the use of this road."

"Joe, don't you remember when they built this trestle? We watched them build it, and we were glad because it would cut two hours off a trip to Kansas City. Do you remember how long it took them to build it?"

"No."

"It took six weeks," Win said. "Six weeks to build, and we just destroyed it in six seconds. We did it to stop the Yankees, but it was our bridge in the first place. The tracks, the bridges, the roads, all these things we are destroying belong to the people of Missouri . . . to us. What kind of war is it when we strike at the enemy by destroying the property of our own people?"

"It's a terrible war, Win, but that's the kind of war we've got," Joe said. "And it's better to destroy one of our own bridges than to give the Yankees one of our towns."

"I understand that," Win said. "But, just because I understand something, doesn't mean I have to agree with it."

"Reveille," Joe said.

"What?"

"Reveille."

"What are you talking about? Since when do Quantrill's Raiders hold Reveille?"

"Reveille!" the conductor called, coming through the car.

Win, who had been sleeping, opened his eyes.

"Reveille!" the conductor shouted again. "Next stop is Reveille, Nevada. Anybody gettin' off in Reveille, this is your stop!"

Win laughed. So, that was how Reveille worked its way into his dream.

He stretched, trying to get the kinks and soreness out. He had been riding a train for three days now, having boarded back in Kansas City, Missouri. It was the first time since the war that he had visited Missouri. And he had made this trip alone, his brother Joe opting not to go with him.

"There's nothing left there for us, Win," Joe had said.

As it turned out, it was a most unsatisfying trip. Joe was right.

"A funny dream?" The voice was soft and melodic, a woman's voice.

"Beg your pardon?" Win replied.

"You were laughing as you awoke," the woman said. The woman was petite, with green eyes, and red curls framing an oval face. Her nose was straight and thin, and her mouth rather full, with ruby lips that were wet and slightly puckered. She was wearing a watch, pinned to her dress as if it were a broach.

"I suppose it was," Win said, not willing to share the real dream with anyone, "but, I've already forgotten it."

He wished he could forget his dreams, but he was cursed to remember, to relive the lingering horrors of a war fought long ago.

"Dreams are sometimes fleeting," the woman said. Smiling, she extended her hand. "My name is Karen McKenzie."

"I'm Win Coulter. That's an interesting watch, Miss McKenzie."

Karen put her fingers on it. "Thank you. It was a gift from my uncle when I came west. I call it my school-marm watch. Will you be getting off at Reveille, Win Coulter?"

"Yes."

"How long will you be staying?"

"I don't know," Win replied. "I'm supposed to meet my brother there. I guess it all depends on when he shows up."

"I hope he doesn't show up too soon."

"Why is that?"

Karen smiled. "Let's just say I am a woman of opportunity. If you have to wait around for a few days, perhaps you will come visit me at The Mother Lode Saloon."

"The Mother Lode Saloon? Isn't it a little unusual for a schoolmarm to spend time in a saloon?"

Karen smiled, but she didn't answer Win's question. Instead, she pulled something from her handbag and handed it to him. "Be sure to bring this with you when you come," she said.

When Win examined the brass coin she handed him, he knew immediately what it was. Called a chit, it was stamped, *Good for one visit.* Such chits were used by prostitutes as a means of payment for their services. The chits were then redeemable for money at the bar. In some towns Win knew the chits were treated as legal tender and could be exchanged for face value at the local bank.

Karen was a whore! He would never have guessed that, and he looked at her in surprise.

Karen chuckled at the expression on his face. "I know, I don't look like a soiled dove, do I?" she asked. "At least, I certainly hope I don't. Not now, anyway. That's because I'm just returning from a visit with my aunt and uncle back in Memphis. They think I'm teaching school out here."

"So, that's what you mean by the schoolmarm watch?"

Karen nodded. "Actually, there is some truth to it. I did start out as a schoolteacher," she explained. "But when the school superintendent's daughter decided she wanted the job, I was fired."

"I'm sorry."

Karen smiled prettily. "Don't be sorry. I'm making a lot more money now and, believe me, I'm having a hell of a lot more fun!"

"You can't make money by giving these things away," Win said, holding up the chit.

"Honey, I don't give them to everyone," she said. "But I was watching you while you were sleeping. You can tell a lot about a man by watching him when he sleeps. I think you would be the kind of customer I like to have. Your first time with me will be free. But all other times . . . and I'm counting on there being other times . . . you will have to pay for the privilege. Call this an advertisement."

"All right," Win said. "I'll take you up on your offer. This may be just the thing to get rid of three days of train weariness."

"For you and me both, honey," Karen said throatily.

The train slowed, brakes squealing, then jerked to a stop. Only three people from the car got up to leave: Win, Karen, and a drummer. The drummer, with cases in both hands, blocked the exit way for a moment, but neither Karen nor Win hurried him. The remaining passengers stayed in their seats, their minds and bodies too travel-weary to pay any attention to the exodus.

Win's first priority, after seeing to his baggage, was to go down to the livery stable to check on his horse. He had left the animal there six weeks earlier when he took the train to Missouri.

"Yes, sir, Mr. Coulter, your horse is doin' fine," the stableman said. "I've fed him every day, let him out for exercise, and rubbed him down."

"Thanks, Charley," Win said. "I appreciate it."

"You were a good customer, payin' in advance like you done," Charley said. "Your saddle and tack are here, too. Will you be leaving now?"

"Not yet," Win said. "I'm going to meet my brother here, so I'm afraid you'll have to put my horse up for a few more days. Do you have the space for him?"

"Sure do, Mr. Coulter. Be glad to have you for as long as you want to stay."

• • •

When Win checked in at the Trojan hotel, he unpacked,
then took a bottle of whiskey from his grip, and poured
himself a generous water-glass full. He drank it without
water, except for the last swallow, which he used to
brush his teeth.

After he was settled in his room, Win went next door
to The Mother Lode. Karen was just coming down the
stairs when he arrived, and the transformation in the
young woman was amazing.

She had been pretty on the train—mousy—but pretty.
Then, she had exhibited the innocence of that breed of
woman that Win often saw but never touched. She
looked as if she belonged to what Win referred to as,
"the other life." The other life consisted of hard-
working, honest men who ranched or farmed, who drove
wagons or stagecoaches, who clerked in stores and
worked in offices. It also consisted of the women and
children who were there in support of those same hard-
working, honest men.

Though Win referred to them as the other life it
wasn't a derisive sobriquet. On the contrary, they were
people he admired, respected, and envied. Win and his
brother lived in a world that was parallel to, but not a
part of, the other life. Had there not been a war, had
things not been so drastically changed by events over
which he had no control . . . he might have been one of
those people, and a woman, such as the woman he had
mistaken Karen for, might be his.

The world in which Win and his brother now lived
was one of transience and a surprising amount of violence. And the women in this life were like the woman
who was now standing the bottom of the stairs smiling
seductively at him. There was very little resemblance
between this woman and the woman he had met on the
train.

Karen's shoulders were bare and she was showing a

generous cleavage through the top of a low-cut, green dress. Her red hair was upswept and jewelry sparkled at the lobes of her ears.

Win walked over to her.

"I believe this is yours," he said, handing her the brass chit.

Chapter 2

JOE COULTER RODE INTO TYBO, NEVADA, LEADING A
pack mule. He was a big man, who right now was wearing a bushy beard and uncustomarily long hair. Almost
two months before, Joe had said good-bye to his brother
at the depot in Reveille, Nevada. Not since then had he
seen civilization, having spent the two months in the
mountains prospecting for gold.

The adventure had produced some results, though
how successful he had been, he didn't yet know. He was
bringing back two saddlebags full of color-showing ore.
Just how well he had done would depend upon the assayer's report.

Tybo was a mining town, with both gold and silver
being dug from the hills. Because of that, Joe's arrival,
complete with pack mule and prospecting equipment,
elicited absolutely no curiosity from any of the citizens.
It was a typical western town, fly-blown, with a single
street, lined on both sides by unpainted, rip-sawed, false-
fronted buildings. It could have been any of several hundred towns in a dozen western states.

As he rode by, a couple of half-naked whores, their
breasts spilling over the top of the chemises they were

wearing, stood on a balcony and called down to him.

"Hey, darlin'!" one of them greeted.

"Just get into town?" the other asked.

Joe smiled, nodded, and touched the brim of his hat by way of returning their greeting.

"Come on up and keep us company. We'll give you a good welcome," one of the whores said.

"Miss, until I get a bath, I'm not even fit company for my horse," Joe said as he rode under her.

The other whore pinched her nose and, exaggerating, made a waving motion with her hand. "Oh, honey, you've got that right," she teased.

Laughing, Joe rode on down the street until he reached a small building at the far end. A sign in front of the building read, "Ronald Dempsey, Assayer."

Joe looked up at the sign, then swung down from his saddle and tied his horse and mule off at the hitching rail. Hefting the saddlebags over one shoulder, he stepped inside. A bell hanging on the front door dinged as he walked in.

"Be right with you," a disembodied voice called from the back of the building. A moment later a small, thin man came into the room. He had evidently been eating his supper, because he was dabbing at his lips with a table napkin. "What can I do for you?" he asked.

"Are you the assayer?"

"Yes, sir, I'm Ronald Dempsey," the little man replied.

Joe lay the saddlebags down on the counter, then opened the flap of one. Several thumb-sized rocks rolled out.

"I need you to take a look at this," Joe said.

Dempsey picked up a couple of rocks, looked at them casually, then put them down. He started to pick up another rock, but then put it down rather quickly and moved his hand to another instead. This rock drew con-

siderably more interest than did the first two he had in-
spected. For this examination, he resorted to a
magnifying glass.

"What do you think?" Joe asked. "Do I have anything
here?"

"You might," Dempsey said, cautiously. He took a
small pick from the drawer and began working on the
rock, chipping off a piece of the color. Then he studied
the color under the magnifying glass.

"Well?" Joe asked.

"It's going to take two, maybe three days before I
have a final answer for you," Dempsey finally said.

"Why will it take that long?"

"I need to be sure," Dempsey replied. "Will you be
staying in Tybo for long?"

Joe scratched his beard. "I had only intended to stay
until I had a bath, a change of clothes, a meal, and a
good night's sleep," he said. "I'm supposed to meet my
brother over in Reveille."

"You could send him a telegram," the assayer suggested.

"Yes, I could do that, I suppose," Joe replied. "But,
why should I?"

"Trust me, Mr. Coulter, it might well be worth your
while," Dempsey said.

Joe thought of the welcome the two whores who
had called down to him gave him as he rode into
town. "I might not mind staying here a couple of days
at that," he said.

The assayer took out a tablet and picked up a pencil.
"Now, what is your name, sir?"

"Coulter. Joe Coulter."

"Have you filed your claim?"

"I did a quick claim while I was up there," Joe said.
"I made a pile of rocks, put my name and the date on a
piece of paper, stuck the paper in an empty bean can,

then buried it. I was told that was all I had to do. Was I told wrong?"

"No, sir, you did all that is necessary for a temporary claim," Dempsey said. "But for something more permanent, you will have to get your file on record. I can do that for you, if you will just fill out this form."

"You think all this is really necessary? I hadn't actually planned to do anything more permanent than scratch around a little and see if I could come up with a couple hundred dollars or so. I figured I would cash that in, then move on."

"Mr. Coulter, you are joking, aren't you?" Dempsey asked.

Joe cocked his head and looked at Dempsey with inquisitive eyes. "What are you trying to tell me, Mr. Dempsey?"

Dempsey took in the handful of rocks that had, thus far spilled from Joe's saddlebags. "Unless I am very, very wrong, I'd say you have at least a thousand dollars' worth of gold just in what you have brought in, in these saddlebags." He reached for the rock that had caught his particular interest a few minutes earlier, then put three or four more with it. "And if there are many more up there like these, you've got yourself a bonanza. Take my advice, Mr. Coulter. Fill out this form and get your claim registered."

"All right," Joe said, filling out the form Dempsey gave him. "You've talked me into it."

"Wait," Dempsey said, scribbling out a note. "If you are going to leave your ore here for me to look at more closely, you'll be needing a receipt." He handed the note to Joe.

"All this says is, received of Joe Coulter, fifteen pounds of mineral-bearing ore," Joe said. "What would keep you from giving me a sack of worthless rocks when I return?"

"I'm an honest businessman, Mr. Coulter, and I would treat you fairly. However, under the circumstances, I don't resent your suggestion. It is good to be cautious." At the bottom of the receipt Dempsey wrote, "Estimated value of ore is one thousand dollars." He signed it, then handed it to Joe. "That's as good as money in the bank," he said.

"Money in the bank, huh? Do you think I could get anything for this note over at the bank?" Joe asked.

"I'm sure you could, but why would you give them any interest? In two or three days the assay will be complete and you can cash this out."

"You are too much the gentlemen to mention it, Mr. Dempsey, but I need a bath and some clean clothes. I'd also like a decent meal and a place to sleep. Right now I don't have two coins to rub together."

Dempsey chuckled. "I understand," he said. "But I'm afraid the bank has already closed for the evening. However, if you don't mind giving me the interest, I'll lend you some money on this ore. How much do you need?"

"Can you go one hundred dollars?" Joe asked.

"I can do that," Dempsey said. On another piece of paper he wrote, "Received on ore, one hundred dollars cash," then he handed it to Joe to sign.

"That little piece you chipped off there," Joe said, pointing to the nugget. "How much is it worth?"

"Gold is forty dollars an ounce . . . this chip weighs six ounces, at least four ounces of which is gold . . . so, this would be one hundred sixty dollars."

"I'd like to keep that too, if you don't mind."

"Be my guest," Dempsey said, handing the small, peanut-shaped nugget to him.

"Guess I'd better tell my brother to join me here. Where is the telegraph office?" Joe asked.

"You'll find it down on the corner," Dempsey said.

"Right next to the apothecary. I think he's closed for the night as well, unless it's an emergency."

"No, no emergency," Joe replied. "I'm just going to tell my brother to meet me here, is all. I can send it in the morning."

Chapter 3

UNDER THE SOFT, GOLDEN LIGHT OF THREE GLEAMING chandeliers, the atmosphere in The Mother Lode Saloon was quite congenial. Half a dozen men stood at one end of the bar, engaged in friendly conversation, while at the other end, the barkeep stayed busy cleaning glasses. Most of the tables were filled with cowboys, miners, and storekeepers laughing over exchanged stories or flirting with one of the several bar girls whose presence added to the agreeable atmosphere.

Because it was mid June, the two heating stoves were now cold, though there continued to hang around these appliances the distinctive aroma of wood smoke from their winter's activity. Mixed with that scent were the smells of liquor, tobacco, women's perfume, and the occasional odor of men too long at work with too few baths.

Win Coulter had been in Reveille for nearly a week now, waiting for Joe to join him. Win's recent trip to Missouri was the longest the two brothers had been separated since the war. With only each other to provide some sense of belonging, Win and Joe Coulter were nomads, moving through the West with no specific purpose and without any particular destination.

During the war, Win and Joe had ridden with Quantrill's Raiders, fighting in the bloody, Kansas-Missouri border campaigns. Though they had also participated in the battles of Wilson's Creek and Shiloh as members of the regular Confederate Cavalry, their guerrilla activity with Quantrill was never forgiven. As a result, in some places of the country, they were still wanted men.

Unlike Frank and Jesse James, and the Younger brothers—colleagues during the war who had turned to the outlaw trail—Win and Joe had managed, for the most part, to avoid any direct conflicts with the law. However, though Win and Joe never looked for a fight, neither did they back away from one, be it with an outlaw or an overbearing peace officer. The very ferociousness with which they settled accounts had brought them a degree of notoriety. Because of that notoriety, as well as their history as riders with Quantrill's Raiders, they were often referred to as the Bushwhackers.

At the moment, however, Win was enjoying the ambience of The Mother Lode Saloon. He was engaged in a game of stud poker with five players he had befriended, including the deputy sheriff, the doctor, and three of the more affluent merchants of the community.

To the casual observer it might appear that Win was so relaxed as to be off guard. A closer examination, however, would show that his eyes were constantly flicking about, monitoring the room, tone and tint, for any danger. And, though Win was engaged in convivial conversation with the others at the table, thanks to his keen sense of hearing, he was listening in on snatches of dozens of other conversations. Additionally, he possessed a sense that could not be described . . . a kinesthesis developed by years of exposure to danger.

"I believe it is your bet, Mr. Coulter," Harley Peters said. Harley was wearing the badge of a deputy sheriff.

Win looked at the pot, then down at his hand. He was showing one jack and two sixes. His down-card was another jack. He had hoped to fill a full house with his last card, but pulled a three instead.

"Well?" Harley asked.

It was easy to see why Harley was anxious. The deputy had three queens showing.

"I fold," Win said, closing his cards.

Two of the other players folded and two stayed, but the three queens won the pot.

"Thank you, gentlemen, thank you," Harley said, chuckling as he raked in his winnings.

"Harley, you have been uncommonly lucky tonight," Doc McGuire said, good-naturedly.

"I'll say I have," Harley agreed. "I've won almost a month's pay."

"We'd better watch out, gentlemen, or Harley will give up the deputy sheriffin' business and go into gambling, full-time," Doc said.

"Ho, wouldn't I do that in a minute if I wasn't married?" Harley replied. "Another hand, boys?"

"Not for me," Win said, pushing away from the table and standing up. "I appreciate the game, gentlemen, but the cards haven't been that kind to me tonight. I think I'll just have a couple of drinks, then turn in."

"What's your hurry?" one of the businessmen asked. "Karen's too busy for you right now."

Karen was, at that moment, engaged in deep conversation with someone at the bar. Part of her job was to work the men for drinks, and she was very good at it because she had a good sense of humor. She had a way of making a man feel important around her, and she seemed to actually enjoy her time with the men . . . with any man.

"Well, she's a working girl," Win said easily. "She has to earn a living like everyone else."

Though Karen had been Win's particular favorite ever

since arriving in Reveille, he wasn't in the least posses-
sive of her, nor did he ever exhibit any sign of jealousy
when she was otherwise engaged. Win's easy attitude
about his relationship with Karen had won friends
among all the men. And, though Karen appreciated the
fact that he held no animus toward her because of her
job, somewhere, deep inside her, a tiny flame of regret
flickered. She would never admit it, even to herself . . .
but she sometimes wished he would show just a little
jealousy.

"I hope you hear from your brother soon, Mr. Coulter," Doc said as Win left the table.

"Oh, I expect he'll be along in another few days,"
Win replied.

"Not too soon, I hope," Harley teased. "I've enjoyed
taking your money."

"I'm sure you have, Mr. Peters, I'm sure you have,"
Win said with a chuckle.

After a couple of drinks at the bar and a few flirtatious
exchanges with one of the bar girls, Win went next door
to the hotel, then upstairs to his room. He lit the lantern
and walked over to the window to adjust it to catch the
night breeze. That was when he saw a sudden flash of
light in the hayloft over the livery across the street. He
knew he was seeing a muzzle flash even before he heard
the gun report, and he was already pulling away from
the window at the precise instant a bullet crashed
through the glass of the window and slammed into the
wall on the opposite side of the room.

He cursed himself for the foolish way he had exposed
himself at the window. He knew better.

There was another shot on the heels of the first, so
close to the first that Win was pretty sure there had to
be two men shooting at him. But he had no idea who
they were or why they were trying to kill him. He
reached up to extinguish the lantern.

"What was that?" someone shouted from down on the street.

"Gunshots. Sounded like they came from the . . ."

That was as far as the disembodied voice got before two more shots crashed through the window. If Win thought the first two shots had cleaned out all the glass he was mistaken, for there was another shattering, tinkling sound of bullets crashing through glass.

"Get off the street!" Win heard a voice, loud and authoritative, floating up from below. "Everyone, get inside!"

Win recognized the voice. It belonged to Deputy Peters, the man with whom he had been playing cards only a few minutes earlier. On his hands and knees so as not to present a target, Win crept up to the open window.

"Harley, stay away!" Win shouted down. He raised up just far enough to look through the window and saw Harley heading for the livery stable with his pistol in his hand. "Harley, no! Get back!"

Win's warning was too late. A third volley was fired from the livery hayloft, and Harley fell facedown in the street.

With his pistol in his hand, Win climbed out the window, scrambled to the edge of the porch, and dropped down onto the street. He ran to Harley's still form, then bent down to check the deputy. Harley had been hit hard, and through the open wound in his chest, Win could hear the gurgling sound of his lungs sucking air and filling with blood.

"Damnit, Harley, I told you to get down," Win scolded softly.

"It was my job," Harley replied in a pained voice. "Coulter . . . the money. See that Claire gets my winnin's."

"I promise," Win said.

At that moment, two more rifle shots were fired from the livery. The bullets hit the ground close by, then ricocheted away with a loud whine. Win fired back, shooting once into the dark maw of the hayloft. Then, leaving Harley, he ran to the water trough nearest the livery, and dived behind it as the assailants fired again. Both bullets hit the trough with a loud thocking sound.

Win could hear the water bubbling through the bullet holes in the water trough, even as he got up and ran toward the door of the livery. He shot two more times to keep the assailants back. When he reached the big, open, double doors of the livery, he ran on through so that he was inside.

"Where'd he go? Critchlow, do you see him?" one of the men in the hayloft called.

"I think he come inside here," Critchlow answered.

Win moved quietly through the barn itself, looking up at the hayloft just overhead. Suddenly he felt little pieces of hay falling on him and he stopped, because he realized that someone had to be right over him. Then he heard it, a quiet shuffling of feet. Win fired twice, straight up, then he heard a groan and a loud thump.

"That's six shots. You're out of bullets, you son of a bitch," a calm voice said. Win looked over to his left to see a man standing openly, on the edge of the loft. The man was holding a rifle and, inexplicably, he laughed. "I ought to thank you for killin' Critchlow like you done. That just leaves more money for me." He raised his rifle to his shoulder, and Win fired.

"What?" the outlaw gasped in shock, dropping his rifle and clutching the wound in his stomach.

"You should have stayed in school," Win said flatly. "Maybe you would have learned to count." He watched as the man fell from the loft, flipping over so as to land on his back in the dirt below. Win walked over to look down at him.

"Coulter! Coulter, are you all right?" It was Sheriff Blaine's voice.

"I'm in here, Sheriff," he said.

Blaine came running in then, puffing from the exertion. He was holding his pistol and he looked down at the body.

"Poor Harley's dead," Blaine said.

"Yeah, I was afraid of that," Win replied. He looked around. "What about the liveryman, Charley?"

"Charley's all right," Sheriff Blaine said. "He was down at The Iron Skillet havin' his supper when all this started. Lucky for him, the way bullets were flying all over the place."

"Yeah," Win replied. He nodded toward the body of the man he had just shot. "Do you know this fella?"

The sheriff rolled the body over with his foot and looked down at it. "I reckon I do. This is Jerry Tombs," he said. "He's a saddle tramp who will do anything for money as long as it's illegal. He normally runs with a man named Critchlow."

Win looked up. "That's the name I heard this one call out. You'll find Critchlow up there."

"What were they after, do you know?"

"They were after me."

"You?"

Win sighed. "This one said that by killing Critchlow, I had fixed it so he would get more money."

"Who's after you?"

"I have no idea, Sheriff. But I guess it could be about anyone. Truth to tell, my brother and I have put burrs under the saddles of more than a few hard hombres over the last several years."

Chapter 4

JOE COULTER WASN'T SURE WHAT AWAKENED HIM. IT was not a slow return to consciousness, for that was a luxury he couldn't afford. Too slow an awakening might mean he would never wake at all. Instinctively, he wrapped his hand around the butt of his pistol. It made no sound as he slipped it from its well-oiled holster.

Moonlight beamed in through the front window, casting indistinct shadows about the room. Joe stared through the shadows, toward where he knew the door to be. The blackness turned to gray as the door opened to reveal a woman. She was carrying a candle, and soft, golden light danced in the silk of her dress.

"Joe?" she whispered quietly.

"Yeah, I'm here," Joe replied. As he slid his pistol back into the holster, it glistened darkly in the ambient light.

"It's me, Lucy. You said come on up at midnight."

Joe sighed and rubbed his eyes.

"You haven't changed your mind, have you?"

"No, I haven't changed my mind," Joe said. Lucy was the friendlier of the two whores who had welcomed him into town when he arrived. After his bath and supper, he was more tired than he thought, and he asked her to give him a couple of hours of rest before she joined him. As he saw her standing there, her features softened by the light, he felt a stirring of interest, indicating that he was rested enough. "Come on in, close the door."

Lucy stepped into the room, then closed the door behind her. The candle cast a little bubble of golden light, bronzing Joe's naked body. Lucy's eyes burned into his flesh.

"Do you always sleep like that?" she asked, as she came over to the bed.

"Whenever I can," Joe replied. "Does it bother you?"

Lucy sat on the side of the bed, then smiling at him, began unlacing the bodice to her dress. "Bother me? No, not at all. In fact, I think it's good. It makes things a lot more convenient."

Lucy, now naked, slid her hand down across the flesh of his belly and into the mat of wiry hair that tangled around the stalk of his manhood. She wrapped her fingers around it, and he remembered then that he hadn't chosen her, she had chosen him. That is, she had been one of the two who had extended a personal invitation to him.

Normally, Joe liked to do his own hunting, but in all the time he had been prospecting, he hadn't so much as gotten one glimpse of a woman. So if, on his first night back in civilization, a good-looking woman threw herself at him, he wasn't going to play hard to get.

Lucy leaned over him, the nipples of her breasts rubbing against his chest as she did so. Smiling, she kissed him, sliding her tongue into his mouth. A fire blazed up in his loins and, putting his hands on her shoulders, he rolled over until she was on the bottom, looking up at him.

He drove into her then, lost to the heat and the passion of the moment.

"Ohhh!" Lucy said through clenched teeth. "Oh, yes!"

Lucy's body bucked beneath his, her eagerness matching his own. Her willing flesh was pliant, and she squirmed as he skewered her to the bed. He reached beneath her and pulled at her buttocks, raising them up as he drove deeper and deeper inside her. Her juices flooded over him, and her thatched nest tugged at him, drawing him into its bubbling secret depths.

Joe went to the pinnacle with her, exploding inside her, spilling hot fluids to gush deep into her as she clutched him desperately in the final spasms of release.

Lucy was still asleep when Joe awoke the next morning. Leaving her in bed, he dressed, then went downstairs.

"Sir," the desk clerk called to him. "My night clerk reported that he saw a young woman go upstairs last night. He believes she went to your room."

"That's right," Joe replied.

The clerk cleared his throat. "Ladies and gents are not allowed in the same room if they aren't married," the clerk said sanctimoniously. "I'm afraid she'll have to leave now."

"We aren't in the same room, because I'm not there," Joe said. "So, leave her alone."

Joe's resolute stare frightened the clerk.

The clerk swallowed a couple of times, realizing then that his throat had suddenly become very dry. "Uh, ve-very good, sir," the clerk finally stammered. "I will allow her to awaken naturally."

"Good man," Joe said. "Now, who serves the best breakfast in town?"

"I believe that would be Little Man Lambert's Cafe, sir, just down the street."

"Little Man Lambert's," Joe said. "Thanks."

"You are quite welcome, sir," the clerk said, looking up nervously toward the upstairs room where he knew a woman was being illegally domiciled.

Before going to breakfast, Joe stopped by the telegraph office to send a message to his brother. A sign on the counter said, "Western Union, Arnold Stone, telegrapher."

"Good morning," Stone greeted Joe as he came in.

"Good morning, Mr. Stone," Joe replied, reading the sign. "I need to send a telegram."

"Well, you came to the right place," Stone joked. "If you had a toothache now, why, you would have to go next door to get a nostrum. On the other hand, anyone going next door to send a telegram would be out of luck." Stone laughed. "Do you want me to write it for you? Or can you write?"

"I can handle it," Joe said, taking the pad.

"Didn't mean any offense. There's lots of folks come in here who can't write," Stone said.

"No offense taken," Joe said easily. Finishing his message, he slid the pad back to Stone. "How long before my brother will get this?"

"Why, no time at all, sir," Stone said. "They have a delivery boy in Reveille, so, like as not, your brother will receive this at his breakfast."

"Thanks," Joe said, paying the rate.

From the telegraph office, Joe went directly to Little Man Lambert's Café. The place was crowded with morning customers, but Joe found a table near the back. As he contemplated his order, he wondered how Win's trip to Missouri had been, though he didn't regret not going. There was nothing back there for them. Their parents were lying in graves, dug on land that was now being farmed by Yankees. The house in which Win and Joe had grown up was nothing but burnt timber and blackened chimneys. Relatives and friends were, for the most part, dead or scattered. There was little chance that anyone was still there. Still, Win wanted to go.

• • •

"Not me. I'm going prospecting," Joe said.

"Prospecting? Prospecting for what?" Win asked.

"I don't know. Gold or silver, I guess," Joe answered. "It's just somethin' I gotta do, Win. I mean, if I don't, I'll spend the rest of my life wondering if there was some big vein out there that I could've found, if I'd just made the effort to look for it. What do you say?"

Win laughed. "I tell you what, Little Brother. You go right ahead," Win said. Win called Joe "Little Brother," because Joe was the youngest, certainly not because of the relative size of the two men. For in fact, Joe was forty pounds heavier and four inches taller than Win.

"And you don't mind going to Missouri by yourself?"

"I don't mind."

The owner of Little Man Lambert's, who, by his size, was appropriately named, approached Joe's table with pad in hand. Though not quite a dwarf, Little Man was less than five feet tall.

"Yes, sir, what'll it be?" Little Man asked.

"You got 'ny flapjacks?"

"Best in Nevada."

"I'll take a dozen flapjacks," Joe said.

"A dozen?" Little Man asked in surprise. "That's a pretty big order. You sure you want that many?"

"Yes," Joe answered.

Little Man chuckled. "All right, friend, if you've got appetite enough to hold 'em, I'll sure cook 'em up for you."

Little Man started to turn, but Joe continued with his order.

"And a rasher of bacon, half-a-dozen sausage patties, and a big piece of fried ham," he added.

"Yes, sir," Little Man said, even more incredulous than before. Again, he started to turn, but Joe still wasn't finished.

"Better bring me half-a-dozen eggs, over easy, a mess of grits . . ."

"I'm sorry, sir, we don't have any grits," Little Man said, interrupting Joe's soliloquy.

"No grits? All right then, bring me some fried potatoes, and, uh . . . you got 'ny gravy?"

By now Joe's rather prodigious order had attracted the attention of others near his table, and nearly all conversation stopped as they listened in on his order.

"Yes, sir, I've got gravy," Little Man said, astonished.

"Good, bring me a pan of biscuits and a side of gravy," Joe continued.

"Excuse me, sir. Where is all this food going?"

"Why, right here," Joe replied, rubbing his stomach, as if surprised by the question.

"You're expecting company?"

Joe shook his head. "Not that I know of. But if someone joins me, be ready to increase the order, would you?"

"Increase the order, yes, sir," Little Man said, now in total disbelief. Little Man stood at Joe's table for several more seconds before he left.

"What is it?" Joe asked. "What are you waiting on?"

"I wasn't sure you were through with your order," Little Man said.

"That's it," Joe said, not picking up on Little Man's subtle sarcasm. "But you might check with me from time to time to see if I need anything else."

As Little Man headed for the kitchen, "to put on another shift," he teased, Joe thought about his brother. It would be good to see Win again, and to find out if there really was anyone left back in Missouri.

If everything went as it should, Win would be in Tybo that evening. Joe imagined that Win would be getting his message, just about now.

Chapter 5

BACK IN REVEILLE AT THAT VERY MOMENT, A PAN OF phosphorous powder flashed as a photographer took a picture of Jerry Tombs and Clyde Critchlow. The bodies of the two dead outlaws, their skin now a pale, blue-white, had been tied into their coffins and propped up against the front of the hardware store. Lucius Pym, the photographer, was doing a booming business by charging citizens twenty-five cents apiece to be photographed standing next to the bodies. For an extra dime he would let them hold a pistol and pose as if they were the ones who had shot the outlaws.

The body of Deputy Harley Peters was being treated with a little more respect. His last mortal remains now lay in repose in the parlor of his own house. His grieving widow was receiving visitors, some of whom had just come from the hardware store where they had gawked at the two men who had killed Harley.

Earlier that morning, Win had given his own condolences to the widow, along with the ninety-four dollars in poker winnings Harley had on him when he was killed. Now Win was in The Iron Skillet restaurant having breakfast.

Cautiously, a young boy came to his table. He wore a pair of gray striped trousers, along with a cap bearing the word "messenger."

"Mr. Coulter?" the boy said.

"Yes?"

"Telegram for you, Mr. Coulter."

"Thanks," Win said. He opened the telegram, then read it as he took a bite of his buttered biscuit.

"WIN. CAN'T COME TO REVEILLE NOW. YOU COME TO TYBO. JOE."

"Will there be an answer, Mr. Coulter?" the messenger boy asked.

"Yes," Win answered. "Send this message. 'ON MY WAY.' "

" 'On my way,' yes, sir."

"Let's see, at ten cents a word, that'll be thirty cents," Win said. He started to hand the boy four dimes, three to pay for the message and one as a tip. Then he drew the fourth dime back and took out a quarter instead. "Would you stop by the stable and tell Charley to get my horse ready?"

"Yes, sir," the boy said, smiling broadly over his good fortune.

Win had a leisurely breakfast with Karen, then checked out of the hotel. Nothing in the telegram indicated he should hurry . . . just that he should come.

Karen waved good-bye to him, then returned to the Double Eagle. Although the saloon was open, there were only two customers in the place and they were the hard drinkers who cared nothing about ambience, girls, or even the quality of their liquor. They came there only to drink.

"Did you tell your friend good-bye?" the bartender asked as Karen passed by.

"Yes, unfortunately."

The bartender chuckled. "I thought you ladies were

never supposed to get too interested in one customer."

"This one was different," Karen said.

Upstairs, Karen looked at herself in the mirror. She was wearing the same dress she had worn on the train, when she first met Win. She put her fingers on her schoolmarm watch and looked at it for a moment. She felt depressed, not only because Win was gone, but because she realized that the life this watch and dress represented were gone too, and could never be reclaimed. With a sigh, she reached for the red satin dress with the daringly low-cut neckline and put it on her bed. This was who she was now.

When she heard the knock, she felt a sudden elation. Win had come back! Smiling, she hurried to the door.

It wasn't Win.

"I don't receive visitors until after six in the evening," she said. Turning away from him, she tried to close the door, but couldn't because he put his foot in the way. "Who do you think you—"

That was as far as Karen got. She suddenly felt strong hands around her neck. She tried to scream, but the crushed larynx prevented that. It also stopped her from breathing.

Win had been riding for eight hours. Behind him, like a line drawn across the desert floor, the darker color of hoof-churned earth stood out against the lighter, sun-baked ground. Before him, the desert stretched out in motionless waves, one right after another. As each wave was crested, another was exposed, and beyond that another still.

The ride was a symphony of sound: the jangle of the horse's bit and harness, the squeaking leather as he shifted his weight upon the saddle, and the dull thud of hoofbeats.

He had filled the canteen before leaving Reveille that

morning. The distance between the two points was sixty miles, all of it through rugged, Nevada desert.

The canteen was already down by a third, and he had been told that there were no dependable water holes between Reveille and Tybo. Already, his tongue was swollen with thirst, but he allowed himself no more than one swallow of water per hour.

Squinting at the sun, he guessed that an hour had passed. He stopped his horse, mopped his brow, then reached for the canteen. He had just pulled the cork when the shot rang out.

The bullet hit his horse in the neck and blood gushed from the wound. Without a sound the animal went down. Win jumped clear to avoid being pinned beneath it. As he did so, however, he dropped the canteen and water began running out onto the hot sand.

Win grabbed the canteen with one hand, while pulling his pistol with the other. He crawled over to his horse and, using it as a shield, looked around to see if he could spot his assailant.

He saw no one.

A moment later he heard the sound of a horse leaving at a gallop. Jumping up, he ran to a nearby rock outcropping then climbed to the top. He saw a lone rider moving fast toward the west. Win aimed at him, then held his fire because the rider was already too far from him for a pistol shot.

Win hurried to his dead horse to get his rifle. The horse had fallen on the rifle and it took Win some time to get it free. By the time he was able to pull the Winchester from his saddle holster, the rider was too far away, even for a rifle. Despite that, Win took a shot at him, more out of frustration than any real hope of hitting him.

"Shit!" Win said, lowering the rifle when, as expected, he missed. "Who the hell is trying to kill me? And why?"

He sat down, puzzled by the sudden interest in having him killed. First, there was that incident back in Reveille. And now, here. Even more puzzling was why the shooter didn't hang around and finish the job? He certainly had the advantage. Win was trapped there, without a horse and with only the water that was in his canteen.

At the thought of his canteen, Win hopped up from the rock and hurried over to check it. There was no sign of the spilled water, as it had already evaporated. He picked the canteen up and shook it, then groaned. It was down to one-half.

Win had a decision to make. He knew he had come at least twenty-five miles since he left Reveille, which meant he had thirty-five miles to go to Tybo. Reveille was south, Tybo was north. The man who had shot at him, however, had gone west. Why did he go west? Win tried to recall the last time he had checked a map. He was certain he had seen no settlement west of the line between Tybo and Reveille. However, if one did exist, it would more than likely be on this side of the mountains, and they were only about fifteen miles away.

If he went west and there was another town, a town he knew nothing about, he would reach it in half the time it would take him to go to either Tybo or Reveille. On the other hand, if he went west and there was no settlement, he would have lost his gamble, and, more than likely, he would die. Win didn't waste time deciding. He took a drink of water—not a swallow, a drink—then he corked his canteen and started west.

It was hard going. An hour or so into his walk, his feet began to swell inside his boots. He picked up needles from prickly pear and once he stumbled over a hedgehog cactus. As the day wore on, he began tiring, and he started breathing through his mouth. The hot, dry air created a tremendous thirst, and the more he thought about it, the thirstier he got. His throat grew more and more parched and his tongue swelled.

He tried to keep up the schedule of one swallow of
water per hour, but he was working much harder now
than he had been when he was riding, and it was nearly
impossible to wait for an hour between swallows. In
addition, there wasn't much water left.

Win had heard that a person could get water out of
some types of cactus. He wasn't sure what kind of cactus
would produce water. He thought saguaro would, but
there was no saguaro cactus in Nevada. A couple of
times he fired a bullet into the barrel of a cactus, then
stuck his finger into the bullet hole to see if he could
find any moisture. He did find a little moisture in one
of them, and he started digging at the pulp, trying to pull
the white, pasty substance through the bullet hole. As a
result, he pierced his hands badly with the needles, but
he did get a mouthful of wet pulp which he chewed. He
also sucked his own blood.

He drank the last of his water at about five in the
afternoon. He started to throw the canteen away, but
decided to keep it in case he did stumble across a water
hole somewhere.

Then, just before dark, a scattering of adobe buildings
rose from the desert floor, wavering in the shimmering
heat waves. The buildings so matched the desert in color
and texture that at first Win wasn't even sure the town
was there. Gathering what strength he had remaining, he
started toward it. He had no choice, now. If it was real,
he would live, if it was a mirage, he would die.

It took him another excruciatingly painful hour to
reach the town. At the edge of town he stopped to catch
his breath and read the sign:

HORSESHOE
POP. 256
"OBEY OUR LAWS, OR PAY THE PENALTY."

Gathering his strength, Win staggered into the little
town. Seeing a pump in the middle of town, he hurried

toward it. He moved the handle a couple of times and was rewarded by seeing a wide, cool stream of water pour from the pump's mouth. Putting his left hand in front of the spout, he caused the water to pool and, continuing to pump, drank deeply. Never in his life had anything tasted better to him.

With the killing thirst satisfied, Win raised up from the pump and looked around the town. Just down the street a door slammed, and an isinglass shade came down on the upstairs window. A sign creaked in the wind and flies buzzed loudly around a nearby pile of horse manure.

These sounds were magnified because the street was silent. No one moved, and Win heard no human voice, yet he knew there were people around. There were horses tied here and there, three of them in front of a building identified by a sign as The Double Eagle saloon.

The thought of a cool beer seemed even more inviting to Win than water, so he started toward it. Just before he got there, though, a man came out of the saloon and stood on the boardwalk.

"Where's your horse, Mister?" the man asked in a voice that sounded a little like a locomotive letting off steam.

"I left him dead in the desert," Win replied. He started forward again, but the man was blocking his way.

"You walked into town?"

"Yes." Win was getting a little irritated. He was hot, tired, hungry, and badly in need of a beer. He didn't feel like explaining everything to this galoot.

The man who was blocking Win's way was a tall man, half a foot taller than Win, taller even than Joe. He was thin and muscular, with a mustache that curved up at each end, like the horns on a Texas steer. He was wearing a yellow duster, pulled back on one side to expose a long-barreled Colt sheathed in a holster that was tied halfway down the big man's leg. He had an angry, evil countenance, and looking directly at him was like staring into the eyes of an angry bull.

"Mister, you're in my way," Win said dryly.

"Would your name be Win Coulter?"

"It is. Why? Do you have a particular interest in me?"

"Yeah, I've got an interest in you." The big man pulled his yellow duster to one side and Win saw a peace officer's badge pinned to his shirt. "I'm arresting you for horse stealing."

"Horse stealing? What are you talking about? I don't even have a horse!"

"You come in here without a horse, that's true," the peace officer said. "But I figure you're plannin' on leavin' with one. So, let's just say I'm stoppin' a horse-stealin' before it takes place."

"Look, I've got no quarrel with the law," Win protested. "But I'm not going back out into that desert. I aim to get myself some supper and a couple of beers, then find someplace to spend the night. Tomorrow I'll buy a horse, then be on my way."

"I'll tell you where you can spend the night. In my jail. You aren't comin' in here."

Win curled his fingers. His hand was so painful and swollen from the frequent encounters with cactus needles that, if it came to a fight, he wasn't certain he could even make a fist. But he wasn't about to let this son of a bitch bully him out of town.

"Time's runnin' short," the lawman said. "What are you goin' to do?"

"I'm going to do just what I told you I was going to do," Win said, speaking slowly and dangerously. He pointed toward the saloon. "I'm going to go in there and get myself some supper and a couple of beers. Now, you can either step aside and let me by, or stay where you are while I come through you."

The lawman made his move then. Win had expected

the lawman to use his larger size to try and enforce his order. To Win's surprise, however, the big man went for his gun.

The lawman was exceptionally quick for his size, and his hand moved toward his long-barreled Colt as quickly as a striking rattlesnake.

Win was caught by surprise. As a result, he didn't even start for his gun until the lawman's gun was coming out. But if Win had been surprised by the sheriff's sudden draw, the sheriff was undoubtedly surprised by Win's speed. Win's draw was smooth and his practiced thumb came back on the hammer in one fluid motion.

In the final analysis, Win may have been given a slight edge by the fact that the Sheriff's gun had an extra long barrel. He had not even cleared leather when Win's finger put the slightest pressure on the hair trigger of his Colt. There was a blossom of white, followed by a booming thunderclap as the gun jumped in his hand.

The sheriff tried to continue his draw but the .44 slug from Win's pistol caught him in the heart. When the bullet came out through the back, it brought half the sheriff's shoulder blade with it, leaving an exit wound the size of a twenty-dollar gold piece.

The sheriff's hand came away from his gun and it slipped back down into his holster as he staggered backward, crashing through the bat-wing doors, and backpedaling into a table before coming down on it with a crunch that turned the table into firewood. He landed flat on his back, on the floor, his mouth open and a little sliver of blood oozing down his chin. His body was still jerking a bit, but his eyes were open and unseeing. He was already dead, only the muscles continued to respond, as if waiting for signals that could no longer be sent.

Win bounded up onto the boardwalk, then pushed through the bat-wing doors, following the sheriff's body inside. A wisp of smoke curled up from the barrel of the pistol he still held in his hand.

There were a dozen people inside the saloon, caught by surprise at the sudden turn of events. They stood there, staring awestruck at the twitching giant of their lawman, lying in the V of the broken table.

Not perceiving any immediate danger from anyone else in the room, Win put his pistol back in his holster.

"Mister, do you know who you just shot?" one of the men in the saloon asked.

"Afraid not," Win said. "We never got around to getting acquainted."

"His name is Luke Taggert. Sheriff Luke Taggert. Never figured anyone would be good enough to beat him."

"He didn't beat him," one of the others said. "Look there. The sheriff's gun is still holstered."

It had all happened so fast, that Win didn't realize Taggert's pistol had fallen back into the holster.

"He started his draw," Win said.

"Uh, huh. And you were so fast you killed him before he could even get his hand to his gun. Is that what you want us to believe?"

"Believe it or not, it is the truth."

"You might be faster'n Taggert, but you ain't that much faster. No one is."

Win didn't like the way this was going, and he started to back out of the saloon. He had taken no more than two steps backward when he felt something cold and hard jam into his back.

"Mister, this here is a double-barreled Greener I'm holdin'," a voice said. "You make one move and I'm goin' to open you up like guttin' a hog."

"You men are making a mistake," Win said. "All I came here for is supper and a couple of beers." He nodded toward the sheriff's body. "This fella threw down on me. I didn't have any choice."

"Let's hang the son of a bitch!" someone called.

"Yeah, somebody get a rope!"

"Hold on, hold on!" the man with the shotgun said. "Bein' as I was Luke Taggert's deputy, I reckon I'm the sheriff now . . . leastwise, till we can get around to another election. And as the sheriff, I say they're ain't goin to be no lynchin'."

"This son of a bitch shot Luke. You aim to just let him walk?"

"It just so happens that the judge is due here tomorrow. I aim to try 'im, then hang 'im legal," the deputy said. He jabbed his shotgun into Win's back, poking him so hard that it nearly knocked the breath from him. "Come along, mister. We ain't that big a town, but we got us a fine jail, thanks to the man you just killed."

Joe was surprised when Win did not arrive that evening. He knew Win had received his message, because Win had answered him, and it wasn't like him to be late. After breakfast the next morning Joe waited anxiously for Win to show. A couple of times he checked the telegraph office to see if there were any messages for him, but nothing was there. When Win hadn't shown by noon, Joe began to worry.

Several scenarios passed through Joe's mind, and none of them were good. He knew Win wasn't lost. And he knew that Win wasn't still in Reveille, for if he had been, he would have sent Joe another message explaining the delay. The most likely thing was that Win's horse had gone down on him. If so, Win would be facing a long walk, maybe with no water.

By one o'clock Joe had made up his mind. With two extra canteens of water hanging from his saddle pommel, he rode out of Tybo, headed for Reveille.

One hour out of town, Joe saw something dark and ominous on the horizon. "Damn," he said aloud. "Get ready, horse. We're about to go through a sandstorm."

The sandstorm hit a few minutes later, and when it

did, it hit with a terrible force. The wind howled like a thousand banshees and sand blew against him with such force that he felt as if it were going to tear his skin off. Tying his handkerchief around his horse's eyes, he led the terrified animal over to a small ridge. There, on the lee side, they waited for two hours until finally, the storm spent its violence.

The storm over, Joe resumed his journey. But, whereas before the desert had texture, now there was none. The desert floor was covered with smoothly rippled sand, much like an open field after a new snowfall.

It was nearly dark by the time Joe discovered the horse. Because of the drifting piles of sand, the animal was nearly buried and Joe almost didn't see it at all. There was no doubt about it being Win's horse. Joe recognized the saddle and tack.

A quick examination of the horse found the bullet wound that killed him. But he saw no other blood on the horse or saddle, so it gave him cause to hope that whoever shot the horse didn't shoot Win.

Joe looked through the saddlebags. He found a small packet of letters that Win was bringing back from Missouri. He read them and for a moment wished that he had gone back to Missouri with his brother. Though their parents had been killed during the war, their mother's sister was still alive and hers was one of the letters.

Also, Joe couldn't help but believe that if he had been with Win, none of this would have happened. Someone might have taken a shot at them, but together the Coulter brothers were so formidable as to be almost invulnerable.

Joe looked around for any sign of a trail. Normally he was a good tracker, better even than Win. But the sandstorm that just passed had completely obliterated any possible trail.

As far as Joe knew, there were two towns in this entire valley—Reveille at the south end, and Tybo at the northern end. Since Win had not been in Tybo when he left, and Joe didn't meet him on the trail, there was only one place he could be. When his horse went down, Win returned to Reveille.

Putting the packet of letters in his own saddlebag, Joe remounted and started riding south.

Chapter 6

"Breakfast," the deputy said.

Win sat up on the bunk and rubbed his eyes. The average man might have found it impossible to sleep while contemplating the thought of a murder trial and hanging, but Win wasn't the average man. He lived a life of such danger that the prospect of sudden death was always in his future. Also, he had arrived in Horseshoe on the edge of exhaustion, so it had been difficult for him to sleep that night.

"Thanks," Win said. He looked toward the tin plate the deputy slid through the door. It contained two biscuits.

"That's it? That's breakfast?"

"That and a cup of water," the deputy said.

Using a tin cup, the deputy scooped some water from a bucket, then passed it through the bars as well.

"Thanks."

There was a pot of coffee brewing on the stove and the deputy poured himself a cup, then looked back at Win.

After his long, dry day the day before, the water wasn't unwelcome. But the coffee smelled exceptionally good and he would have liked some. He would be damned before he asked for any though.

"Damn, this coffee is good this morning," the deputy said, smacking his lips in appreciation.

Win knew that the deputy was riding him, but he said nothing. Instead, he just returned to his bunk and began eating his biscuits and drinking his water.

The deputy tried a couple more times to get a rise from Win, but had no more success than he did with the coffee. Finally he got up from his chair and walked over to look through the bars.

"What's it feel like to know you're goin' to die?" he asked.

"We're all going to die," Win replied. "It's just a matter of when. A hundred years from now, the worms will be finished with both of us."

The front door to the jail opened then, and a rather robust, bearded man wearing a suit came in. The deputy turned toward him, then smiled broadly.

"Good mornin', Judge," he said. He pointed to the cell. "We got you a prisoner to be hung."

"We are going to try him first," the judge said. He looked pointedly at Win. "Then we'll hang him."

"Yes, sir, that's what I meant to say," the deputy replied, his voice reflecting his toady deference.

The judge walked over to the cell and looked through the bars at Win. "I am Judge Preston Coit," he said to Win. Then, over his shoulder, he called back to the deputy. "Mr. Elam, do you know who we have here?"

"Who?" Elam asked.

"We have Win Coulter of the Coulter brothers."

Win was surprised, not only that Coit knew he was a Coulter, but that he knew which one he was.

"They are called The Bushwhackers, and no worse pair of murdering scoundrels have ever terrorized society," Coit said.

"Is that a fact? Is there a reward out for them?" Elam

asked excitedly. " 'Cause, if there is, I caught 'im." The deputy hurried over to the desk, then started looking through all the reward posters.

"You won't find anything," Win said.

"He's right," Judge Coit said, turning away from the cell. "There are no dodgers out for the Coulters. At least, none that I know of."

"I thought you said they was murderers," Elam said.

"They are," Judge Coit insisted.

"How do you know that, if there ain't no posters out on them?"

"I know, because I know," Coit said. "What is today?"

"Today is Wednesday, June nineteenth," Elam answered.

"All right, we'll hold the trial on Friday, the twenty-first. Foster will prosecute. Davenport will defend."

"Davenport? You mean Dexter Davenport? Judge, you're kiddin' ain't you?

"I never 'kid,' Mr. Elam. I assure you, I am quite serious. Where would Mr. Davenport be right now?"

"More'n likely, he's sleepin' off last night's drunk some'eres," Elam replied. "Prob'ly over in the livery. Gordon lets him stay there."

"Get him. Tell him I will expect him in court this afternoon, prepared to defend this prisoner."

"Judge, ole Davenport ain't drawed a sober breath in two years, let alone made an appearance in court. Ever since . . ."

"I'm well aware of Dexter Davenport's travail," Coit said, interrupting Elam in mid-sentence. "I realize things have not gone well for him of late. But as a qualified attorney, he has no choice but to accept this assignment, or I will jail him for contempt of court and disbar him for life."

"You're goin' pretty harsh on him, ain't you, Judge?"

"Just find him," Judge Coit ordered.

• • •

Dexter Davenport awakened to the smell of horse manure. He was used to the smell, sleeping in the livery as often as he did, but this morning it seemed much stronger than usual. When he opened his eyes, he saw why. Too drunk last night to realize what he was doing, he had gone to bed in a pile of the stuff. It was all over him, and he began scraping it off.

"Davenport? Davenport, you in here?"

"I'm back here," Davenport replied.

Deputy Elam came back to him, then stopped several feet away. "Son of a bitch!" Elam gasped. "Damn, you stink." He waved his hands in front of him.

"Yes, well, I wasn't all that particular about where I slept, last night," Davenport answered. "What is it, Deputy? What do you want?"

"I don't want nothin'. It's the judge that wants you."

"Judge Coit?"

"Yeah, he's over to the sheriff's office now. He wants you to defend a prisoner."

Davenport shook his head. "I don't practice law anymore. Judge Coit knows that."

"That may be, but he asked me to find you."

"Very well, Mr. Elam, you have found me. Now, go back and tell the judge that I have no intention of trying a case in my present condition."

"You got to," Elam said. "The judge said if you don't, he'll throw you in jail for contempt, then have you dis . . . dis . . . something or the other."

"Disbarred?"

"Yeah, I think that's what he said."

"Yes, that sounds like something Judge Coit would do." Davenport looked down at himself. "I can't see the judge looking like this."

"He didn't say nothin' 'bout how you was s'posed to look. He just said fetch you back to him, and that's what I aim to do."

Davenport scraped off as much of the greenish-brown

goop as he could, then nodded at the deputy. "All right," he said. "Let's go see the distinguished jurist."

"The what?"

"Judge Coit," Davenport said.

"Yeah, let's go. Only, stay upwind of me."

Coit took one look at and one whiff of Dexter Davenport then ordered him to take a bath and get on clean clothes before presenting himself.

"It costs a quarter to take a bath," Davenport said. "And three dollars to get my clothes out of the boarding-house. Missus Johnson is holding them in lieu of my bill."

"I'm authorizing payment of twenty dollars to serve as public defender," Judge Coit said. "Here's five dollars in advance. Come back when the smell of you doesn't sicken a pig."

"Yes, sir," Davenport mumbled.

Elam chuckled as Davenport left. "Hey, Coulter, did you see that man?" he called.

"See him? For a moment, I was afraid he would be sharing a cell with me," Win answered.

"Sharing your cell? No, it's better than that," Elam said. "Davenport is a lawyer. Fact is, he's your lawyer." Elam whooped with laughter.

When a well-dressed and rather dignified man stepped into the sheriff's office an hour later, Elam didn't recognize him.

"Yes, sir, something I can do for you?" Elam asked.

"Don't you recognize me, Deputy? It is I, Dexter Davenport."

Elam's eyes grew wide. "Well, I'll be damned. It is you," he said.

Davenport nodded toward the cell. "I would like to speak with my client."

"Sure, go right ahead."

"Alone," Davenport said.

"Alone? What do you need to see him alone for? Hell, just go over there and talk to the son of a bitch."

"Article fifteen, paragraph six, slash, b of the Nevada law code says that defense council will be given a room to have private consultations with their clients. Since you have no such place, that means you must step outside," Davenport said.

"To hell with that. There ain't no drunk goin' to tell me what I got to do."

"I can get a court order from Judge Coit to order you to do so," Davenport said.

Elam glared at Davenport for a moment, then, with a sigh, took his hat down from the peg and jammed it onto his head.

"All right," he said. "I'll give you your time." He nodded toward the street. "I'll just be out there if you need me."

"Thank you, Deputy. I won't be needing you," Davenport said.

Elam nodded once, then looked back toward the cell and Win.

"All right, Coulter. Here's your lawyer. Better talk fast, while he's still sober." Elam laughed at his own joke as he stepped outside.

Davenport went over to the stove and with shaking hands poured himself a cup of coffee. Then, without being asked, he poured a second cup and carried it over to the cell to pass between the bars. His hand was shaking so that some of the coffee was splashing out.

"Better get it while there's some left in the cup," Davenport said, making a bitter joke at his own expense.

"Thanks," Win replied.

Davenport pulled a chair over and sat down, just outside the cell. He studied Win over the rim of his cup as he took another swallow. "They didn't tell me your name," he finally said.

"Coulter. Win Coulter."

"Mr. Coulter, I'm Dexter Davenport . . . and I am your court-appointed attorney."

"My court-appointed attorney?"

"That's right, sir. Of course, you don't have to accept me. You can hire your own."

"Are there any other attorneys in this town?"

"Only one, and he will be prosecuting," Davenport replied.

"Are you really an attorney?"

"Yes, sir, I am, duly qualified before the bar."

"You'll forgive me for asking, but when I saw you earlier, you didn't exactly look like a lawyer," Win said.

"That is very true. I have been besieged by demons, as it were, for some two years now. But I assure you, I am a qualified lawyer, and I will do all I can for you. Now, if I may ask, with what crime are you charged?"

Win looked at Davenport in surprise. "You are my lawyer and you don't even know that?"

"I know nothing about you or the charge, Mr. Coulter," Davenport replied. "My introduction to this case occurred approximately an hour and a half ago, when deputy Elam pulled me from a pile of horse shit where I had spent the night." Davenport looked around the office. "By the way, where is Sheriff Taggert? I haven't seen him yet."

"Well, you've asked two questions," Win said. "But I can answer both of them at the same time. The reason Taggert isn't here is because he is dead. And the reason I am here, is because I am the one who killed him."

Davenport had been slouching in the chair. He sat up quickly when Win said he had killed Taggert. The expression on his face was one of shock.

"You killed Taggert? How?"

"He braced me as I was going into the saloon last night," Win said. "We had a few words and the next thing I knew, he was going for his gun. I had no choice but to kill him."

"You say he was going for his gun, but you still managed to shoot him?"

"Yes."

Davenport shook his head. "Mister, you are either incredibly fast or a bold-faced liar. And it doesn't make any difference which one you are because the jury is never going to believe anyone was able to beat Sheriff Taggert on the up and up."

"What about you? Do you believe me? I mean, if you are going to be my lawyer, you have to believe me, don't you?"

"No, sir, I don't have to believe you to represent you," Davenport said. "But I understand now, why Judge Coit chose me to defend you."

"Why?"

"It is Coit's penchant for irony, Mr. Coulter," Davenport said as he got up and walked back over to the coffeepot to refill his cup. Using both hands to steady his cup, he took another drink. "Yes, sir, I imagine he is having quite a laugh over this . . . as is Taggert . . . if there is such a thing as laughter in hell," he added.

Chapter 7

JOE'S FIRST STOP WHEN HE REACHED REVEILLE WAS THE telegraph office.

"Yes, sir, you want to send a telegram?" the telegrapher asked, stepping up to the counter. He was a small, bald man who kept his thick glasses on by way of a black ribbon which stretched from earpiece to earpiece around the back of his head.

"No, thanks," Joe answered. "But I'm looking for someone who has recently sent a telegram from this office. His name is Win, and he stands about this high." Joe held his hand out four inches below the top of his own head. "Weight wise, I'd say he dresses out around a hundred and eighty pounds or so. His hair is light and his eyes are blue."

"Mister, you don't have to describe Win Coulter to me, or to anyone else in this town," the telegrapher replied. "Not after what happened Saturday night."

"What happened?"

For his answer, the telegrapher slid a copy of the local newspaper across the counter.

GUNFIGHT HURLS THREE MEN
TO ETERNITY

**Deputy Harley Peters Killed, His Widow Mourns
Jerry Tombs and Clyde Critchlow Also Slain
World Is Better Off for Their Demise**

Saturday night, at fifteen minutes of
eleven o'clock, the streets of Reveille
became a battlefield when four desperate men threw themselves at each
other in deadly struggle. At last, when
the smoke had cleared, only one, Win
Coulter, remained alive. By his courage, and the accuracy of his shooting,
the murder of Deputy Harley Peters
was avenged, and two of the most per-
nicious desperadoes ever to walk the
streets of Reveille were dispatched to
their Maker, whose mercy they can
only hope for, as no one who remains
on this mortal coil would deign to lift
a prayer on their behalf.

Joe read the article, then looked up from the paper.

"Yes," he said. "That would be Win. Do you know
where I can find him?"

"You won't find him in Reveille. He has gone up to
Tybo to meet his brother," the telegrapher said.

"I am his brother, Joe. And I did send a telegram
asking him to come. He answered that he was on his
way, but he never got there."

The telegrapher clucked his tongue and shook his
head. "Oh, dear," he said. "The country between here
and Tybo is most inhospitable. I do hope nothing bad
has happened to him."

"I thought perhaps he might have come back to Rev-

eille," Joe said. He didn't tell the telegrapher about finding Win's horse.

"Well, if he did, you might ask Mr. Bascom. He's the
clerk at the Trojan Hotel. That's where he was staying."

"Thanks," Joe said.

The Trojan hotel was bracketed by two saloons,
O'Toole's on the right and The Mother Lode on the left.
If he found out nothing at the hotel, he would ask in the
saloons.

There was a small lobby just inside the door of the
hotel. The lobby was furnished with one, well-worn,
horsehair sofa and a scarred rocking chair. A brass spittoon occupied the space between the chair and the sofa.
A threadbare carpet covered the floor. In the corner was
a cast-iron stove, cold now, in the summer months. The
smokestack was removed and the flue cover on the
chimney was decorated with a painting of bright red
flowers.

To the right of the door as he came in was a counter
that divided the lobby from the office area. On the left
wall just beside the counter was a cabinet of cubbyholes,
each hole containing the room key. One or two of the
cubbyholes had envelopes in them. The back wall was
dominated by a large clock, its face divided by Roman
numerals. The pendulum swung in a measured arc, each
movement emitting a loud tick-tock.

The hotel clerk was not wearing a jacket. The long
sleeves of his striped shirt were gathered with garters,
just above the elbows. Wearing a bolo tie and bright
orange suspenders, he was eating an apple as he stepped
up to the desk.

"You would be Bascom?"

"I am, sir. What can I do for you?"

"I need to see your guest book," Joe said. "I'm looking for Win Coulter."

"Mr. Coulter stayed with us for nearly a week, but he
checked out Sunday morning."

"And you're sure he didn't come back?"

"I'm positive he didn't come back. I would have known."

"Is there another hotel in town?"

"We are the only hotel of any consequence," Bascom said smugly.

"Thanks," Joe said, disappointed. His hope was that somehow Win had made it back to Reveille. It appeared that Win hadn't come back at all. Or if he had, he had not returned to the hotel.

"Will you be wanting a room, sir?" the clerk asked.

Joe hadn't come to the hotel with the intention of taking a room, but it was too late to do any more traveling that night, so the idea suddenly sounded good to him. "Yes," he said. "Yes, I believe I will take a room."

"Very good sir. And your name?"

"Coulter. Joe Coulter."

"You are related to Mr. Win Coulter?"

"He's my brother," Joe explained. "We were supposed to meet in Tybo, but he never showed."

"I can understand now, your interest in him," the clerk said. He nodded toward one of the saloons. "If it is of any help to you, Mr. Coulter, he spent a good deal of time in one of the saloons. As I recall, he seemed to prefer The Mother Lode."

"Thanks," Joe said. He paid for the room, but didn't go up right away. Instead, he went next door to The Mother Lode to follow up on the lead.

As far as small town saloons went, Joe thought The Mother Lode was fairly nice-looking. It sported a real mahogany bar. A mirror behind the bar was bracketed by a shelf that was filled with scores of bottles of various kinds of liquor and spirits. A sign on the wall read: "Gentlemen, kindly use the spittoons."

"What'll it be, gent?" the bartender asked, sliding down the bar with a towel tossed across his shoulder.

The fact that the towel was relatively clean spoke volumes about the class of the establishment.

"Beer," Joe replied. "Do you serve eats?"

"Bacon, beans, biscuits," the bartender replied.

"I'll take it," Joe said. Scooping a couple of boiled eggs from the large jar that sat on the end of the bar, Joe took them and his beer over to a nearby table. It didn't take long for one of the bar girls to approach him.

"Hello," she said, smiling her greeting at him. "My name is Alice."

Alice was tall, raw-boned, and full-breasted. She had wide set, blue-gray eyes, high cheekbones, and a mouth that was almost too full. She was the kind of woman that Joe found most desirable, and of all the bar girls present, she was the one who left the pack to greet him. It was as if such women had a sixth sense and knew intuitively they were the kind of girl he was attracted to.

"I don't think I've seen you in here before," Alice said.

"Just got into town," Joe answered. He kicked a chair out by way of invitation, then nodded at the bartender. The bartender brought Joe a second beer, as well as a drink for the girl, even though the girl hadn't ordered.

"He must know your brand," Joe said.

"One glass of tea is pretty much like any other glass of tea," Alice said with unaccustomed candidness. She picked it up and held it toward Joe in a toast. He laughed, then touched his beer to her glass.

"Well, at least you're honest about me paying whiskey prices for your tea."

"Honey, if everything we drank really was whiskey, we'd all be soused by seven every night," Alice explained. "And what good is a soiled dove, if she's passed out drunk?"

Joe laughed. "I can see your point," he said.

"So, what brings you to Reveille?" Alice asked.

"I'm looking for someone."

"Seems like everybody is looking for someone or something," Alice said. "Who are you looking for?"

"I'm looking for my brother, Win Coulter."

"You're Win's brother? Then you must be Joe."

"You know him then? I see that I came to the right place."

"You came to the right place, all right. I'm glad to see that the two of you came back. Especially after what happened. Are you supposed to meet him in here?"

Joe shook his head. "*We* didn't come back."

Alice looked confused. "What do you mean? You're here, aren't you?"

"I am, but Win isn't. He never showed over in Tybo. When I came back along the trail looking for him, I found his horse, dead. But there was no sign of my brother. He didn't go on to Tybo, and now it looks like he didn't come back this way, either."

"Couldn't you track him?"

Joe shook his head. " 'Fraid not. A big sandstorm came up and blew away all the tracks. By the way, what do you mean after what happened?"

"With Karen."

"Karen?"

"Karen took a particular shine to your brother, and I think he liked her."

"Where is she? I would like to talk to her."

"Just a minute," Alice said. She walked over to the bar and said something to the bartender. The bartender nodded, then reached under the bar and came up with a newspaper, which he handed to Alice. Alice brought the paper back to the table.

"Maybe you should read this," she said, handing the paper to Joe.

"Yes, the telegrapher showed me the story about the shooting that Win was in. I've read it."

"No," Alice said. "Not that story. This story." She pointed to another story at the bottom of the page.

WOMAN FOUND STRANGLED

Karen McKenzie Killed in Her Room
Sheriff Blaine Has No Suspects

Karen McKenzie, a popular soiled dove who plied her avocation at The Mother Lode Saloon, was found strangled in her room on Saturday last. She was last seen alive at about eight-thirty that morning by Bill Bean, the bartender at The Mother Lode and by two customers.

Though Sheriff Blaine has no suspects, he believes robbery may have been the motive. A broach watch, which belonged to Miss McKenzie, has not been found. It is thought that the killer may have strangled her, then took the watch as payment for his grizzly deed.

"It says here that there are no suspects," Joe said as he finished the article. "Has the sheriff come up with anyone since the article was written?"

Alice shook her head. "You know, when someone goes into 'the life,' real people forget all about us. In many cases, even our families turn their backs on us. So, when something happens to one of us, like what happened to Karen, it doesn't mean much. Nobody cares about a dead whore."

"That's not true," Joe replied. "If Win knew about this, he would care. I care, and I never even met her."

"You and your brother are exceptions then," Alice said. "I hope you find your brother, but his chances aren't very good, are they? I mean, if you found his horse dead, that means he's on foot, wandering around out in the desert."

"The chances aren't good for an ordinary man. But Win's not an ordinary man, so I'm not ready to count him out, yet."

As he ate his supper, Alice told Joe all she knew about Win. She pointed out some of the men with whom Win had played cards and, after his supper, Joe talked to them as well.

All wanted to share the story of Win's participation in the shoot-out that some insisted would make Reveille famous. But no one was able to shed any light on anything that may have happened to Win. They did express some concern over the fact that Win had lost his horse during the trip.

"The desert between here an' Tybo ain't where a man on foot needs to be," one of them said.

None of the men even mentioned Karen McKenzie, giving some credence to Alice's comment that nobody cares about a dead whore.

Joe left The Mother Lode at about nine-thirty, then went over to O'Toole's to check it out. O'Toole's was a saloon that catered to the rougher trade. It had none of the niceties of The Mother Lode, no tables, no mirror behind the bar, and no girls. The bar itself was made of rip-sawed, unpainted pine. The drinks were cheaper, and the whiskey raw. Joe didn't have to hang around there. He knew this wouldn't be one of Win's regular haunts.

When Joe stepped back out into the street, he felt their presence before he heard or saw them. Two men with knives jumped from the dark shadows between the buildings, and only that innate sense which allowed him to perceive danger when there was no other sign saved his life. Because of that, Joe moved out of the way of the attack at the exact moment the two men started it,

so that their knives, swinging in low, vicious arcs, did
not immediately disembowel him.

Despite the quickness of his reaction, one of the
knives struck him, and as Joe went down to the street,
rolling to get away from them, the flashing blade opened
a wound in his side. The knife was so sharp and so
adroitly wielded that Joe barely felt it. He knew, however, that the attack had drawn blood.

For all their skill with the blades, the assailants had
made a big mistake. Both of them were wearing light-
colored shirts and trousers, so that notwithstanding the
darkness of the street, they were easy to see. One of the
would-be assassins moved quickly to finish Joe off before he could recover, and that was the attacker's mistake. Joe twisted around on the ground, then thrust his
feet out, catching the assailant in the chest, driving him
back several feet. The other one moved in, keeping Joe
off his feet, keeping him away from his gun.

The assailants were good: skilled and agile. But they
were small, giving Joe a little advantage, though his size
was nearly overcome by their quickness. Joe sent a
booted foot whistling toward one of them, catching the
man in the groin. Then Joe came up off the ground,
ramming stiff fingers into one of the men's eyes as he
did so.

The man screamed, dropped his knife and reached up
to his face.

The other one, the one who had been sent back by a
kick in the chest, grabbed his partner, and pulling on
him, broke off the fight.

Joe felt the nausea rise up in him. Bile surged in his
throat. Dizzy, he staggered over to The Mother Lode,
then went back inside. All conversation stopped at his
entrance, and the silence lingered like a leaden weight
over Joe's head. Everyone stared at him with curiosity.
This time, their mouths opened in shock.

Joe didn't realize it, but he was quite an apparition to

behold. He stood there, just inside the swinging bat-wing doors, ashen-faced, holding his hand over a wound which spilled bright red blood between his fingers. He surveyed the room for just a moment, then, with great effort, walked to the bar.

"Whiskey," he ordered.

The solemn-faced bartender poured him a glass and Joe took it, then turned around to face the silent patrons. By now his side was drenched with blood from his wound, and the blood was beginning to soak into the wide planks of the floor.

"Joe!" Alice said, moving to him quickly. Joe held his hand out to keep her away.

"If any of you had anything to do with me getting knifed, I'm going to give you fair warning. The next man who even looks at me cross-eyed, I'm going to pull him apart with my bare hands." Joe looked at them, tossed down the drink, then set the empty glass on the bar. After that, he walked calmly from the bar. With each passing moment, he was growing more dizzy and more light-headed from the loss of blood. When he reached the entrance to the saloon, he stuck out one hand to grab the door frame. He struggled to steady himself as he walked out of the saloon.

Joe started toward the hotel, only this time he moved far enough away from the buildings so that there was no chance of anyone else jumping him from the shadows. He moved out into the middle of the street and lurched along with a stumbling, staggering gait, trying to stay on his feet, though his head was now spinning so badly he could barely stand.

When he finally reached the front of the hotel he fell against the door, managing to keep on his feet, then stumbled through. He knew he had to get off his feet quickly, so he lurched toward the stairs to keep from falling on the floor.

"Mr. Coulter!" Bascom called, startled by Joe's unusual entry. "Mr. Coulter, are you all right?"

"I'm fine," Joe said. "I'm just fine."

Joe leaned against the wall beside the stairs for a moment to get his breath, and when he did so, he left a stain of his blood. Then, holding his side, he climbed the stairs to his room. Once inside he ripped the bedsheet in two and wrapped it around his side, pressing it tightly against his wound. When the crude bandage was in place, he fell across the bed, closed his eyes and passed out cold.

Chapter 8

DEXTER DAVENPORT WAS JUST FINISHING HIS MEETING with Win, when the man Judge Coit had chosen as prosecutor arrived. Foster swept into the sheriff's office, dressed in tails and a stove-pipe hat, while carrying a silver-headed cane. He wore a diamond stickpin in his cravat and silver links at his cuffs. A gold watch chain stretched across the silk vest, accenting his rather considerable girth. His hair was neatly trimmed, as was his Van Dyke beard.

"Good morning, Mr. Davenport," Foster said.

"Good morning, Mr. Foster."

"May I interview the prisoner? Or do you require a little more time?"

"He's all yours," Davenport said, starting toward the door.

"You are welcome to stay while I talk to him," Foster said. He put his cane and stove-pipe hat on the sheriff's desk.

"Thank you, no, I . . . uh . . . have some business to attend to."

"To be sure. Well, you go right ahead, Mr. Davenport," Foster said.

"Davenport," Win called as Davenport started through the front door. Davenport turned back toward him. "Will you be sober when I see you next?"

"A good question," Davenport replied. "And under the circumstances you are entitled to an honest reply. Well, here it is, Mr. Coulter. It is certainly my intention to be sober when you see me next, and I am going to try. But I can't promise you."

Win nodded. "If I can't have sobriety, Mr. Davenport, then I will settle for honesty," he said.

Foster chuckled as Davenport left the office. "You may just have given him permission to get drunk again."

"Mr. Davenport is an adult," Win replied. "If he wants to get drunk, he certainly doesn't need my permission."

"To be sure, to be sure," Foster said. He cleared his throat. "Mr. Coulter, my name is Brigham Foster, and I am here to prosecute you. I don't suppose there is any need in telling you that you are in a great deal of trouble."

"I sort of figured that out," Win said.

"You can save yourself some trouble by confessing."

"Confessing what? That I killed Taggert? Hell, I did kill him."

"I mean confessing that you drew first, that there was no gunfight as you claimed, and that you killed him with malice and aforethought. Come clean with that, Mr. Coulter, and you could save us all a lot of trouble."

Win chuckled. "What about the hangman? Would I save him trouble as well?"

Foster shook his head. "Since you prize honesty so, I'll be honest with you. The only trouble you will save, is the trouble of a trial. There is no plea bargain being offered. I'm afraid Judge Coit plans to hang you no matter what."

"Then I may as well stick to my story."

"Let me get this straight. You story is that Taggert started to draw on you . . . whereas you, seeing the sheriff start his draw, commenced your own draw, and beat him. And, you not only beat him, you were so fast that when he came crashing backwards through the door into the saloon his pistol was still in its holster. Is that about it?"

"That's it," Win said.

Foster clucked his tongue and shook his head. "Mr. Coulter, do you have any idea how ridiculous that claim is? Taggert was, by all accounts, incredibly fast with a gun. Now . . . while it is possible that someone may have been faster—perhaps even you—it is highly unlikely that anyone would be so much faster that Taggert's gun would still be sheathed."

"It doesn't look good, does it?" Win asked.

"No, sir, it doesn't look good at all. As a matter of fact, it is the most far-fetched thing I could possibly imagine."

"Nevertheless, that is what happened," Win insisted.

"So, you are sticking by your story?"

"I reckon I don't have any choice, since what I'm saying is true," Win said.

Foster walked back over to the sheriff's desk and picked up his hat and cane. He put his hat on his head, then squared it, before he turned to look back toward Win in the jail cell.

"Have it your way, Mr. Coulter," Foster said. "It was my intention to spare you the indignity and humiliation of a public trial, but you spurned my offer."

Win laughed. "The indignity and humiliation of a public trial? You just told me the judge plans to hang me no matter what. What could be more undignified and humiliating than a public execution?"

"I'll see you in court," Foster said. "Good day, Mr. Coulter."

After Foster departed, Win stood at the bars of his cell for a moment looking over the empty room, studying every aspect of it. Directly across from him, and running parallel with the cell, was the front wall. The door was in the center of the wall, with a window on either side. The windows were dirty, with half their openings masked by window shades of dark green. The wall to his right had another window and a large board to which were posted dozens and dozens of Wanted Posters.

The poster board was obviously not kept up-to-date, for Win recognized one of the wanted men as someone he had killed more than two years earlier. As he studied the other posters, he realized that he had run across several of the others as well, for both Win and his brother lived the kind of lives that brought them in frequent contact with such men.

There was also a calendar on the wall. The picture on the calendar was of a passenger train, roaring through the night with sparks spewing from the smokestack and steam streaming from the cylinder. Every window of every car was glowing with light.

On the calendar page, every day had been X'd out until the current day, which was Wednesday, June nineteenth. Win heard the Judge say he wanted the trial to be held on the twenty-first. He couldn't help but wonder if he would still be alive by the twenty-second.

Where was Joe? Was he still waiting for him in Tybo? Knowing Joe, Win doubted very much if he was. Joe had probably come looking for him and, if so, would have found, not only his horse, but his tracks leading here. Joe would find him, Win was certain of that. Joe could track a fish through water.

As Win stood at the bars of his cell, musing over his situation, the front door opened again. Hesitantly, a young woman stuck her head through the door.

"Deputy Elam?" she called.

"He isn't here," Win said.

"Are you Win Coulter?" the girl asked.

"Yes."

Nervously, the girl brushed a fall of hair back from her forehead and walked over to the cell. Although she was a blonde, her eyes were deep brown. It was an unusual and very attractive combination. "Would you come closer please?" she asked.

Win, who was already standing next to the bars, wondered just how much closer he could get. She answered his question for him when she stuck her arm through the bar, put her hand on the back of his neck, and pulled his face toward her. Through the bars, she kissed him full on the mouth.

Win was startled by the young woman's unexpected move but it wasn't at all an unpleasant surprise.

When she pulled away from him she looked up at him with her large dark eyes.

"Thank you," she said.

"One little kiss isn't much to thank a man for," Win replied. "If I ever get out of here, maybe I can do something that really earns your thanks."

For just a moment the girl looked baffled, then suddenly she laughed.

"I wasn't thanking you for the kiss," she said. "The kiss was my way of thanking you."

Now it was Win's time to be confused. "Thanking me for what?" he asked.

Win had never seen anyone's face transformed as quickly as did the young woman's. The smile left her lips and her eyes narrowed with loathing.

"For killing Luke Taggert," she said.

"Yes, well, I'm glad it earned your approval," Win said. "But I have to tell you, it wasn't anything I planned. It just happened."

"I don't care how it happened. As long as he is dead."

"Even if I hang for killing him?"

Before the girl could answer, the front door to the jail opened and Dexter Davenport came in. He was carrying a couple of books with him, and when he saw the girl, he looked surprised.

"Sue, what are you doing here?"

"I came to thank Mr. Coulter for doing what nobody else in this town had the courage to do."

"He needs more than thanks," Davenport said.

"Put me on the stand," Sue said. "Let me tell my story."

Davenport shook his head. "That would only complicate things," he said. "Mr. Coulter claims that Taggert drew first. If you tell your story, it might suggest to the jurors that Coulter planned to kill Taggert. It could even plant the idea that you paid him to kill Taggert."

"I would have paid him to kill Taggert. I would have paid anyone to kill him if I had thought I could find such a person."

Davenport nodded. "Uh, huh. Do you see what I mean? Believe me, having you take the stand would only make matters worse. Let the court handle it."

"That's what you told me two years ago."

Davenport nodded. "It wasn't the court who failed you then, darlin'. It was me."

"If that's true, you can make it up to me now," Sue said.

"How?"

Sue looked back toward Win. "Get this man off," she said.

Davenport held up one of the two books he was carrying. "I've been working on that," he said. "I may have found a way to keep him from hanging."

Sue shook her head. "I don't mean just keep him from hanging," she said. "I mean, get him off. I want him to go free."

"You're asking for a miracle," Davenport said.

"You owe me a miracle," Sue replied coldly.

Chapter 9

SHORTLY AFTER JOE STAGGERED OUT OF THE MOTHER
Lode, Alice went into the kitchen of the saloon where a
medical kit was kept. She got a roll of bandages, some
salve and crushed aloe leaves, then sneaked out the
back door, and down the alley, to the back of the hotel.
Slipping in through the back door of the hotel, she
walked quickly through the hallway until she reached
the lobby. Bascom was reading a *Police Gazette*. He
looked up when Alice came in.

"Hello, Alice. Do you have business over here tonight?" Bascom asked. He looked at her lustfully. He
had once offered her a deal. He would make a room
available for her for any business she might want to
conduct "off the books" of the saloon. In return, she
would provide him with her services.

Alice declined the offer, but Bascom never stopped
thinking about the possibilities.

"No. I just stepped out for some fresh air and I
thought I would come in and say hello to you. It's been
a while since you stopped by for a drink."

"Yes, well, uh, Mrs. Bascom doesn't really approve,"
Bascom said.

Alice leaned over the counter, affording him a magnificent view of her cleavage. When his eyes went there, as she knew they would, she managed to reach around the corner and take the skeleton key from its hook. With that key she could open any door in the hotel.

"Oh, that's such a shame," Alice said. "The girls all enjoy your company so. One of them asked me just the other day if I thought you would ever come back."

"Really? Which girl?" Bascom asked, his voice dripping with lust.

"I think it was Linda," Alice said. There was no girl named Linda, but Bascom didn't know that.

"Linda, yes! Tell her . . . tell her I'll be by to see her soon," Bascom said excitedly.

"I'll do that. Well, I must go back to work. Good-bye."

"Good-bye, Alice," Bascom said.

Alice had accomplished two things by her conversation with Bascom. Out of the corner of her eye, she had checked the register to see that Joe Coulter was in room 201. And, she had managed to secure the pass key.

Alice walked back to the front door. She opened it, then looked back at Bascom, who had already returned to the *Police Gazette*. She closed the door, then stepped behind a large, potted plant. Studying Bascom through the leaves, she waited until he got up and walked to the back of his office to pour himself a cup of coffee. That gave her the opportunity she was looking for, and she slipped quickly and quietly up the stairs to the landing on the second floor.

A moment later, she slowly and quietly let herself into Coulter's room. With her heart pounding fiercely for the risk she was taking, she closed the door behind her, then stood for a moment in the dark shadows, letting her eyes adjust to the darkness.

The room was hot and sticky, and she could smell the blood from Joe's wound. She felt around in the dark until she found the bedside table and lantern. Finding a box of lucifers, she struck one, then held the flame to the wick as she turned up the fuel. A golden bubble of light pushed away the darkness.

Because of the wound, Joe was in a much deeper sleep than normal. He neither heard Alice when she came into his room nor did he awaken when she lit the lantern. It was only when she sat on the bed beside him that his eyes snapped open. Even then, he awoke more from curiosity than from a sense of danger.

"What?" Joe asked. "What are you doing?"

"Shh," Alice whispered, holding her finger across her lips. She began unwinding the sheet from around his side. "I'm going to treat your wound," she said.

"It'll be all right."

"No. It must be cleaned and treated," Alice insisted. "I have bandages and medicines."

"All right," Joe said with a sigh. "I never argue with a beautiful woman who is treating me well." He lay back on the bed.

Alice had the sheet completely unwound now, and she sucked in her breath as she looked at the blood which had coagulated around the wound.

"You've lost a great deal of blood," she said. "You're lucky you aren't dead. Who did you make mad?"

Joe chuckled. "I don't have the slightest idea. Oh, it hurts when I laugh." He laughed again.

"Be still now," Alice said as she poured water from the porcelain pitcher into the basin. "I'll clean your wound, then dress it."

Joe lay back down and folded his hands behind his head. The muscles in his arms, shoulders, and chest rippled as he did so, and he looked up at the beautiful young woman who brought the water to the small table and sat again on the bed beside him.

"All right, I'll be still," he promised.

Gently, Alice began cleaning the blood from Joe's

side. The cut started just above the belt line and disappeared below the waistband of his pants. Alice unbuttoned his trousers, then slipped them down. The hair which began as a tiny dark line at his navel broadened into a dark, curling bush. She stopped there before any more was revealed.

"Thank heaven the cut didn't go deep enough to damage any of your innards. But you have bled a lot."

Joe looked directly into her eyes and saw a latent smoke of lust in their depths.

For reasons she couldn't explain, Alice felt a tremendous heat suffusing her body as she cleaned him. She was a prostitute, a woman who had seen many men. And yet there, in the innocence of that room, the situation seemed different. As if mesmerized, she slowly pulled Joe's trousers a little farther down, though not all the way. It was almost as if she were a young virgin girl, seeing a man for the first time, and she sucked air audibly through her teeth.

"You . . . you are a handsome man," she said quietly.

Alice felt Joe's abdomen. It was incredibly hot, perhaps fevered by the wound, and yet she could feel the pulsing of his blood just beneath the skin. Though it wasn't necessary for her to pull his trousers the rest of the way down, she did. As she bathed him, she bent over and the top of her blouse fell forward, exposing the curve of her breasts. She felt a heat there, then looked up to see that Joe was looking at the view she had presented him. She smiled, almost shyly, and continued to work.

When his wound was completely clean she applied a salve to it, then rubbed on the crushed medicinal herbs. "Does it feel good?" she asked.

"Yeah," Joe croaked.

Alice finished applying the medication but she let her hand continue to rub his skin. Her hand moved in ever-widening circles until finally she reached his penis. She squeezed it, feeling it grow in her hands. She smiled down at him.

"I think maybe I should take care of this, too," she said.

"Lady, you'll get no argument from me," Joe said huskily.

Alice peeled out of her blouse, then stepped out of her skirt. She stood in the candlelight beside the bed, displaying her full, beautiful body to him. The taut nipples glowed in the light, while shadows kept mysterious the promise of her thighs. She sat back on the bed and looked at him.

"But you are wounded," she said. "Perhaps you can't make love while you are wounded."

"We'll find a way," Joe said.

"Yes, we'll find a way," Alice agreed. She leaned down and kissed his neck, then started working her way down his chest. Joe could feel the soft, velvet heat of her darting tongue as she licked his skin, trailing back and forth until she stopped at his nipple and flicked her tongue over it several times.

Joe tried to move over her, but the pain stabbed at him. When Alice saw that, she smiled gently, put her cool fingers on his shoulders to indicate that he should stay where he was, then moved over him, straddling him and taking him into her, orchestrating the moment for both of them.

Joe felt Alice over him, pressing down against his thrusts, making love to him. He felt her jerk in wild spasms as the jolts of rapture racked her body. With a groan, she fell across him, even as he was spending himself in her in his final convulsive shudders.

They lay that way for several moments with Alice on top, allowing the pleasure to slowly drain from her body. Finally she got up and looked down at him. She licked her lips and they glowed in the gleam of lantern's light.

"I am a prostitute," she said. "I have done this many

times, with many men. But never before have I done it
because I wanted to."

"And you wanted to with me?"

"Yes."

"Why?"

"I . . . I don't know why," Alice said. She reached
down and touched his penis. It was slack now, spent of
the energy which had lifted it moments earlier. "Never
before have I felt what I felt with you, Joe Coulter." She
looked at the cut, noticing that their lovemaking had
opened it up a little. "Oh," she said. "I'm sorry. I have
made it worse."

Joe chuckled. "Believe me, it was worth it."

"I will clean the wound again, and this time I will
bandage it."

Joe put his hand on Alice's naked thigh. "Don't bandage everything," he teased. "I might have use for it
again."

Alice smiled. "You are quite a man, Joe Coulter," she
said.

She didn't leave Joe's room until just before dawn.

Chapter 10

ON THURSDAY MORNING, JUNE TWENTIETH, A TALL, skinny, scarecrow of a man came into the jailhouse. He was carrying two coils of rope and a can of beeswax. He put the rope and can on the corner of what had been Sheriff Taggert's desk, then looked back toward the jail cell.

"Is that fella there my customer?" he asked Elam.

"Yes, sir, Mr. Tatum, that's him, all right," Elam replied. "His name is Win Coulter."

Tatum walked up to the jail cell and looked over at Win, who was lying on the bunk with his hands folded behind his head.

"Mr. Coulter, my name is Amos Tatum. It's going to be my privilege to be your hangman. Yes, sir, I'll be tellin' my grandchildren that I was the one that hung Win Coulter. Now, get up, boy. Get up an' let me take a look at you."

Win did no more than glance over at him. He made no effort to get out of his bunk.

"I said, get up," Tatum repeated.

Win remained motionless.

"Well, you can suit yourself," Tatum said. He took

out a small pad and a pencil. "It ain't really goin' to change nothin', 'cause I can get quite a bit of information just by lookin' at you there. 'Course, it's to your advantage that I get it all right. If I make a mistake you could either wind up chokin', real slow . . . or else havin' your head pinched right off whenever you drop through the trap."

"Aren't you jumping the gun a little there, Mr. Tatum?" Dexter Davenport asked, coming into the office just as Tatum was making his last comment.

"What do you mean?" Tatum asked.

"You're talking about hanging a man who hasn't been found guilty. In fact, my client hasn't even been tried."

Tatum laughed. "He's your client? And you're telling me he hasn't been found guilty yet?" he asked. "That's a good one." Tatum chewed on the end of the pencil with his teeth, exposing a little more of the pencil lead. "Now, let's see . . . I'd make you about five feet ten, maybe five-eleven."

Win offered no response as Tatum wrote the numbers in his book.

"And, I'd say, a hundred seventy, maybe a hundred seventy-five pounds. Of course, that's before you're served your last meal," he added. "Some folks eat so much at their last meal they mess up all my cipherin'." He laughed at his joke.

"You don't have to be worryin' none about this fella eatin' too much," Elam called over from his desk. "All I've give him to eat so far, is biscuits and water."

Davenport looked back toward Elam with a frown on his face. "Is that right? You've given this man nothing but biscuits and water?"

"Yeah. The way I look at it, why waste money on him? I mean, if we're only goin' to hang him, anyway."

"Is that what the judge ordered?"

"Judge don't have nothin' to do with feedin' my prisoners. I do," Elam said.

Davenport looked at Win. "Why didn't you tell me about this?" he asked.

"I didn't figure I was going to starve in three days," Joe said. "And I figured you had enough on your mind without worrying about whether or not I was getting anything to eat."

"Get this man a meal," Davenport ordered.

Elam bristled. "Look here, you ain't nothin' but a lawyer . . . and a drunken one at that. You got no say-so whatever on how I treat my prisoners."

"I said get this man a meal," Davenport demanded. "Or I will take this to the judge and you'll be looking for another job . . . that is you'll be looking for another job as soon as you get out of jail."

"Jail? What do you mean, jail? Why would I be goin' to jail?"

"Mistreatment of your prisoners is a jailable offense," Davenport said. He smiled. "In fact, I might even be able to arrange for you and Mr. Coulter to share the same cell."

"All right, all right, I'll go down to Ma Putnams' place an' get 'im some bacon and beans," Elam said, grumbling. He slammed the door behind him as he left the office.

"What are you trying to do, Dexter?" Tatum asked as he continued to make entries in his small notepad. "Cheat me out of my hangin' fee? If you get this fella off, I don't get paid."

"I intend to get him off if I can," Davenport said.

"I thought you gave up the lawyering business."

"No, I, uh, turned my back on it for a while. But I didn't give it up."

"Is that a fact? Well, tell me, Dexter, how long have you been sober?"

"Twenty-six hours and," Davenport looked up at the clock, "fourteen minutes," he concluded.

"That long? Well, I'm just real proud of you, Dexter.

Are you having a hard time with it? I'll bet you'd like a drink now, wouldn't you?" Tatum started yanking open the drawers on Elam's desk until he found what he was looking for. He held up a bottle of whiskey and read the label. "Old Overholt," he said. "Well, now, that's not exactly the brand they serve in the finest establishments, is it?" He looked over at Davenport. "But then, you haven't been all that choosy of late, have you?"

Davenport rubbed the back of his hand across his mouth. "I . . . I don't want that," he said.

"Oh, sure you do," Tatum replied in an oily-smooth voice. He found a glass that was half full of water, tossed the water out on the floor, then poured in about two fingers of whiskey. He looked at it, then shook his head. "Nah . . . that's not enough. Not for someone who has been dry for as long as you have." He poured the glass nearly full, then held it out toward Davenport. "Here you go," he said.

Davenport stood absolutely motionless for a long moment, staring at the glass. Win, who had not yet risen from the bunk, watched the drama being played out before him, but he offered no comment.

"I . . . I said I don't want it," Davenport stammered.

"Yes, I heard what you said. Tell you what I'm going to do. I'm just going to set this glass over here, on the corner of the desk. That way, if you really don't want it, why, it's over here out of harm's way, so to speak. On the other hand, if you need just a small drink to get you through all this . . . and, believe me, that is perfectly understandable . . . well, it'll be right here for you."

Chuckling, Tatum picked up one coil of rope, then uncoiled it. He sat down in the empty chair behind what had been Taggert's desk, and started applying beeswax to the rope. "Yes, sir," Tatum said. "I'll just leave that glass over there while I grease up the rope, make it slide real easy. We want the knot to break his neck. Like this."

He made a circle with his thumb and forefinger, then slipped it down the rope as if it were the knot sliding. When he reached the end, he made a clucking sound, then tilted his head abruptly as if the neck had just been broken. "Otherwise, ole Coulter there would just sort of dangle at the end of the rope, chokin' to death, real slow."

"One drink," Davenport suddenly said, starting toward the glass. He had been staring at it ever since Tatum put in on the desk. "One drink won't hurt me. I need it. I can't think without it."

Fifteen minutes later, Elam returned with Win's food. He took it over to him.

"Here," he said. "And I recommend that you enjoy it. This time tomorrow, you'll be eating supper in hell. What do you think about that?"

"I think the company in hell will be an improvement over what I've seen in Horseshoe," Win replied. He took the tin plate, then returned to his bunk. Sitting on the edge of his bunk, he ate the food ravenously.

Elam looked around the office, surprised to see that no one was there.

"What happened to Dexter and the hangman?"

"They had business elsewhere," Win replied, not looking up from his plate of beans.

A short time later the front door was pushed open and the woman Win knew only as Sue, came in. "He's been drinking again," she wailed.

"Who? You mean Davenport?" Elam replied.

"You know full well who I mean," Sue said. "You gave him whiskey. Why? Why did you do that? Were you afraid he'd prove himself in court tomorrow?"

"Wait a minute now. You just hold on there, Missy," Elam said, holding his hands out in front of him. "I didn't do no such thing. Last time I seen him, he was sober as a judge. Fact is, he made me go get somethin' for the prisoner to eat. Where's he at, anyhow?"

"I took him up to his room, half-drunk," Sue said. "He says he started drinking over here."

"The hell he did. I told you, last time I seen him, he was sober."

"Is that true, Mr. Coulter?" Sue asked.

"What the hell? You goin' to take a murderer's word over mine?" Elam asked.

"The deputy is right," Win said.

Surprised at being vindicated by Win, the deputy looked toward his cell. " 'Course, on the other hand, I reckon it's all right to take his word for it when he's tellin' the truth."

"Are you telling me he wasn't drinking over here?"

"No, I'm not telling you that," Win said. "I'm just saying that the deputy had nothing to do with it. The hangman searched around until he found a bottle. That was all it took."

"Ohh," Sue groaned. She went over and sat in the chair behind Taggert's empty desk, then hung her head. "I thought . . . that is, I hoped . . . things would be better now."

Chapter 11

JOE HEARD A DRUM POUNDING AND HE WONDERED WHO would have a drum and why they would be beating it. Then he awakened and realized that it wasn't a drum, it was someone banging on the door to his room.

"Coulter! Coulter, are you in there?"

Slowly, wincing at the pain in his side, Joe sat up. The room was redolent with Alice's musky perfume, even though she was gone.

"Coulter!"

Joe slipped his pistol from the holster then moved painfully over to the door.

On the other side of the door the pounding grew more desperate.

"Coulter, this is Sheriff Blaine. If you are in there, answer me!" the voice called from the other side of the door.

Without saying a word, Joe jerked the door open. That left him standing there with the drop on the sheriff, who had just raised his hand to knock again.

"What do you want?" Joe asked.

The sheriff smiled, self-consciously. "Well, I reckon you just answered that for me," he said.

"What do you mean?"

"I understand you were jumped by a couple of men last night. I just wanted to see if you was still alive."

"I'm still alive," Joe said. "Are you disappointed?"

"Disappointed? No, not at all. I hate it when someone in my town gets killed, unless I'm the one doin' the killin'. It just causes more work for me," Blaine said.

"Yeah, well, I'm glad I didn't cause you any more work," Joe said.

"Do you need tendin' to?"

"I've been tended to."

The sheriff looked at the clean, neat bandage on Joe's side.

"I see," he said. "Looks like whoever did it did a pretty good job."

"I've got no complaints," Joe said. "And I particularly liked the bedside manner."

Sheriff Blaine looked at Joe with a confused expression on his face, then he shook his head. "I'm not even going to ask about that," he said. "Seems to me like you and your brother have made some pretty powerful enemies."

Joe perked up. "Have you heard from my brother? Do you know where he is?"

Sheriff Blaine shook his head. "Sorry, I don't have any idea where he's at. Last thing he told me was he was goin' over to Tybo to meet you."

"Yes, that's the last thing he told me, too. Wait a minute, what do you mean, my brother and I have made some pretty powerful enemies?"

"The two men your brother killed? They started the fracas by trying to kill Win. Now, you come to town, you're here less than one day, and from what I hear you didn't rile anyone in particular. Yet, last night two men tried to kill you. Why?"

"I don't know."

"They are after you and your brother, but you don't know why?"

"No."

"Too bad. I was hoping you might be able to shed a little light on what's going on around here. What are your plans now?"

"Now?" Joe replied. "I plan to eat breakfast."

Fifteen minutes later, Joe and Sheriff Blaine were having breakfast together.

"Did you know my brother? Did you meet him before he had the run-in with Tombs and Critchlow?" Joe asked.

"Oh, yes, I met him. He came in on the train about a week ago. He hung out over at The Mother Lode Saloon . . . mostly playing cards, sometimes keeping company with that woman who got herself killed."

"You are talking about Karen McKenzie."

"Yes," Blaine said.

"Do you think there could be any connection between Karen getting killed and people who are trying to kill my brother and me?"

Blaine stroked his chin for a moment as he pondered the question. Finally, he shook his head. "No, I don't see how there could be," he said. "I'm pretty sure whoever killed that girl, killed her for that watch she was always wearin'. 'Course, that means her killer has long since left these parts. He couldn't very well sell that watch to anyone around here, since ever'one knows that it belonged to the McKenzie woman."

"Maybe one of Karen's customers was jealous of Win," Joe suggested. "Maybe the same person who tried to kill Win is the one who killed Karen."

Sheriff Blaine shook his head. "No, I don't think so. From what your brother said, someone hired Critchlow and Tombs to try and kill him. Normally, people who kill out of jealousy do it themselves."

"Yeah, I guess that's right. I'm just trying to find a reason for all this, that's all. You said Win played a lot of cards. Did he win big?"

"You mean did a sore loser hire Tombs and Critchlow to kill him?" Blaine asked.

Joe nodded.

"It doesn't seem likely. Your brother had one pretty good night at cards, but from what I've heard, the other nights were pretty even. And the last night he was here, he even lost a few dollars. At any rate, there wasn't enough money changed hands in any given game to cause anyone to be all that upset. Besides which, the fellas he played cards with are all upstanding citizens. I'm sure none of them had anything to do with it."

"Then what is it? Why did someone try to kill him?"

"You tell me, Mr. Coulter. Whatever it is, it's pretty obvious the trouble didn't start here."

"You say that, Sheriff, but Win was attacked here, and so was I. Nothing happened to me while I was in Tybo."

"Listen, are you sure your brother didn't make it to Tybo? Maybe he did and you just missed him over there."

"I know he didn't make it. Because when he didn't show up, I started backtracking, and I found his horse out on the trail."

"What happened to the horse?"

"Someone shot it."

"Maybe Win shot it his ownself. Maybe his horse stepped in a hole or something and Win—"

"No," Joe interrupted. "There was nothing wrong with the horse except for the bullet hole in his neck. It was a rifle bullet. A 44-40."

"Did you look around?"

"I looked, but I couldn't track him because a sand-storm took out all the tracks. I figured he either had to go on through to Tybo or come back here to Reveille."

"Well, I'm absolutely positive he didn't come back here," Blaine said. "We're a small enough town, and Win made himself well enough known in that shoot-out that, if he had come back, I would know it."

"He didn't go to Tybo, either," Joe said. "And I'm sure he didn't wander off into the desert. He's much too smart for something like that. And I know he didn't disappear into thin air."

"Maybe he went to Horseshoe," Sheriff Blaine suggested.

Joe looked up from his breakfast in surprise. "Horseshoe? Where is Horseshoe? I've never heard of it."

"It's about halfway on a line between here and Tybo, though maybe twenty miles to the west. The three towns make a triangle in Hot Creek Valley."

"Are you sure there is such a place?" Joe asked. "I didn't see it on the map."

"Of course it's on the map. It's . . . wait a minute, what map are you talking about? Let me see it. Do you have it with you?"

"No. But there was a map on the wall of the bank over in Tybo. I checked it over pretty good before I came here."

Sheriff Blaine grinned. "The McGruder map. I should've thought of that."

"The McGruder map?"

"McGruder is an engraver from San Francisco. He does maps for such places as banks, saloons, railroad depots and the like. They are for show. They aren't meant to be used for anything more than that. Didn't you notice all the artwork? The mountain lions, the lizards, cactus, old, abandoned mines, and the like? He even draws little trains on the tracks between the towns. Only, sometimes, if something gets in the way of one of his pictures—a town for instance—why he'll just leave it out. On the latest map he drew, he left out the town of Horseshoe. Instead, he drew a picture of a cloud, complete with a face and pursed lips blowing wind. The thing is, those maps are everywhere, and lots of people take them for real."

"Yeah, like I did," Joe said disgustedly. "Horseshoe, huh? Thanks, Sheriff, you've been a big help." He left a coin on the table beside his plate, then he stood up.

"Where are you going?" Blaine asked.

"I'm going to Horseshoe. Win has to be there."

"That's a pretty long ride," Blaine said. "There's an easier way to find out than by going there."

"How's that?"

"Simple. I'll wire the sheriff and ask him if he's seen Win."

"You know the sheriff over there?"

"Yeah," Blaine said. "I know him. I don't like the son of a bitch, but I know him. He's always been a particular favorite of the district judge, Judge Coit. With any other judge, Taggert would have probably been jailed a long time ago for being too quick with his gun."

"Can you trust him?"

"I wouldn't trust him any farther than I could throw him if he had any personal stake in the matter," Blaine admitted. "But as far as just providing information on whether or not your brother might be in Horseshoe, well, I can't think of any reason why Taggert would lie about it. Come on, we'll send a telegram over there and see if they've heard anything."

Joe walked down to the Western Union office with Sheriff Blaine, then stood by as Blaine wrote out the message. He handed the message across the open counter to the telegrapher.

"Get this over to Sheriff Taggert in Horseshoe," Blaine said. "And ask for an immediate reply. We'll wait right here for it."

"Oh, my, you still haven't found your brother, Mr. Coulter?" the telegrapher asked. "Well, I'll get this right out and see if we can get some word for you."

"Thanks," Joe said.

Joe leaned up against the wall with his arms folded across his chest as he watched the telegrapher's fingers operate the key. There were several clacks going out, then, a moment later, the key began clacking on its own. Joe realized that it was an incoming message from the other end, and he walked over to be there when the message ended. It wasn't a very long message.

"Odd," the telegrapher said.

"What's odd?"

"The message just says, 'unable to deliver.' "

"They don't tell you why?"

"No, sir."

"Raise 'em again. Find out why,"

Again the key clacked with both the outgoing message, and the incoming. With a face devoid of all expression, the telegrapher wrote out the message as it came in, then he handed it to Blaine. He glanced, once at Joe, as Blaine read the message.

"What is it, Sheriff?" Joe asked. "What does the message say?"

"Sheriff Taggert's dead," Blaine said. "He's been murdered."

"Murdered?"

"That's what it says here."

"Damn. So we still don't know if Win is there."

"Oh, he's there, all right," Blaine said.

"What? He's there? How do you know?"

Without a word, Blaine handed the telegram to Joe.

"SHERIFF TAGGERT MURDERED BY ITINERANT NAMED WIN COULTER. TRIAL AND EXECUTION SET FOR TOMORROW."

Chapter 12

"OYEZ, OYEZ, OYEZ, THIS COURT IS NOW IN SESSION, draw near all who have business with this court, the honorable Judge Preston Coit presiding. All rise."

Coit, wearing a robe, came into the courtroom and took his seat. Amidst the sound of scraping chairs and the rustle of pants and dress fabric, the gallery also sat. A spittoon rang with the quid of a well-aimed expectoration.

Court was being held in the town's all-purpose community room, which was utilized for everything from town meetings, to dances, to church revivals, to its current use as a courtroom. Though not designed specifically as a courtroom, it was far superior to some of the other places that were put to that use in small, western communities, such as schoolrooms or even saloons.

Coit stared out over his desk at the two tables that had been placed in front of the room, one for the prosecutor and one for the defense. At the prosecutor's table he saw Brigham Foster busily arranging his notes. At the defense table Win Coulter was sitting alone.

"Did you dismiss your counsel, Mr. Coulter?" Judge Coit asked.

"No."

"Where is he?"

"I don't know. I haven't seen him this morning," Win replied.

Coit glared at Elam. "Mr. Elam, I deem it your responsibility to have counsel present when trial begins. Counsel is not present, therefore I am fining you five dollars."

"Judge, that ain't fair," Elam protested. "Like as not, the son of a bitch is off drunk some'eres. I don't know why I should be held to blame."

"Make that fine ten dollars, Mr. Elam," Judge Coit said. "Do you care to go on?"

"No, Your Honor," Elam said contritely.

"I didn't think so. Now, please go find him, and bring him here."

"Yes, Your Honor," Elam said.

Coit turned toward the prosecutor's table. "Mr. Foster, you may present your opening comments."

"Wait!" a female voice called, rushing in through the back door, just as Elam was leaving. There was a buzz of surprise from this unexpected interruption, and Coit looked up with an obvious expression of irritation on his face.

"Who called out?" Coit asked.

"I did, Your Honor."

When Win turned to see who it was, he saw that it was Sue, the same young woman he had met, the day before.

"And you are?"

"You know who I am, Your Honor."

"Yes, Miss Davenport, I know who you are. But I want you to state it for the court record," Coit said, patronizingly.

"I am Sue Davenport, daughter of the defense counsel."

That was a surprise to Win, but what came next was an even bigger surprise.

"And co-counsel for the defense," she added.

"*You* are co-counsel?"

"Yes, Your Honor."

Judge Davenport stroked his chin. "I knew that you had been reading the law with your father," he said. "But I wasn't aware that you had passed the bar."

"I haven't passed the bar, Your Honor. But according to the Nevada Code, if I have the defendant's acquiescence, and your permission, I can act as co-counsel."

"I see," Davenport said. He looked over at Win. "Tell me, Mr. Coulter. Do you give this girl permission to act as your co-counsel?"

"Why not?" Win replied. "At least she is sober."

The courtroom erupted into laughter, but Coit's gavel quieted them.

"I'll have none of that in my court," he said. He addressed Sue. "Girl, where is your father?"

"He'll be here shortly," Sue replied. "He was unavoidably detained."

"Unavoidably detained," Coit repeated.

"Yes, Your Honor."

Coit looked at Sue for a long time then, finally, nodded his head. "Very well, Miss Davenport, you may act as co-counsel."

"Thank you, Your Honor. And I have an immediate objection."

"You have an objection? What could you possibly be objecting? The trial hasn't even started."

"Yes, sir, it has," Sue insisted, speaking, even as she was walking up to take her position at the defendant's table. "As I was entering the courtroom, I heard you invite Mr. Foster to present his opening comments. But there has been no *voir dire*."

"Mr. Foster and I have already taken care of that," Coit said. "We questioned the jurors quite thoroughly this morning, and found them acceptable. I acted on your father's behalf, since he wasn't present."

"But surely you can't—"

"Your objection is overruled, Miss Davenport. If defense counsel had wanted to be present for *voir dire*, one of you had every opportunity to do so. Since neither of you showed up, I took the responsibility of conducting *voir dire* for you. Now, Mr. Foster, you may present your opening remarks," Coit said.

"Thank you, Your Honor," Foster said. He stood up and looked over toward the jury. "Gentlemen of the jury, today you are going to be asked to undertake an awesome responsibility. You are going to be asked, not only to pass judgment on a fellow human being, but to sanction the taking of that man's life on this very day, by way of hanging.

"However, when I present all the facts in this case, the defendant's callous disregard for the code by which we all live, as well as the eyewitnesses to this cold-blooded murder, then you will have no personal difficulty in bringing forth a verdict of guilty and assessing the punishment as death." Foster paused for a moment, then looked over toward Win before his dramatic conclusion. "Death by hanging," he said.

"Defense?"

"What?" Sue asked, looking up as if distracted.

"Do you have any opening comments, Miss Davenport?" Coit asked.

"Uh, no, Your Honor. Defense has no opening comments."

"Very well. Prosecution, you may proceed with your case."

"Are you just going to sit there and say nothing?" Win whispered.

"I've never tried a case before," Sue replied. "But I know that sometimes it's better to say nothing, than to say the wrong thing. I'd rather leave all that to my father."

"Yes, your father. Where is he?"

"He, uh, had a difficult time last night. It is taking him a while to pull himself together this morning."

"You mean he is hung over," Win said.

"He is making an effort, Mr. Coulter. If only you knew what an effort he is making. He will be here. He promised me he would, and I believe him."

"I admire your loyalty, Miss Davenport, but the truth is, I'm probably better off with him absent."

"No, you're not. My father is a good lawyer. I will admit that he has fallen on some bad times, but he is a good lawyer."

Foster stood then, to call his first witness.

"Your Honor, although I have depositions from half a dozen who were present when Sheriff Taggert was shot, I am only going to call Jed Murphy. I do that because all of their testimony is virtually the same. Should defense counsel wish to question any of the others, prosecution has no objections."

"Call your witness, Counselor," Coit said.

"Prosecution calls Mr. Jed Murphy."

Jed Murphy was a man of average height and weight. He was about thirty-five, though a lifetime of hard work made him look older. He raised his right hand to be sworn.

"You swear to tell the truth, the whole truth, and nothing but the truth, so help you God?" the clerk asked.

Murphy spit a wad of tobacco into the spittoon, then wiped his mouth with the back of his hand before he answered.

"I do."

During the questioning that followed, Murphy told how he had been standing at the end of the bar nearest the door. He heard a shot from outside, and, turning, saw Taggert staggering, back-pedaling through the bat-wing doors. He fell on a table, by his weight and the force of his fall, broke it into two pieces, then wound up on his back, on the floor.

"Did Sheriff Taggert say anything?" Foster asked.

"No, he was deader'n shit by the time he hit the floor," Murphy said.

There was a tittering of laughter from the gallery.

"You say your heard a shot from outside. How many shots did you hear?"

"One."

"Only one shot?"

"That's all."

"Is it possible that there were two shots, but fired almost simultaneously, thus giving the illusion of one shot?" Foster asked.

"I don't know how that could be."

"Why is that?"

"Taggert didn't even have his gun out. It was still in the holster when he hit the floor."

"Thank you, Mr. Murphy. I have no further questions."

"Miss Davenport?" Coit asked.

As Sue approached the witness, Murphy turned toward the judge.

"Judge, are you goin' to let this here girl ask me questions like she was a lawyer?"

"As far as you are concerned, Mr. Murphy, she is a lawyer," Coit replied. "And you will answer accordingly."

"Yes, sir. Well, I'll say this. I ain't never seen a prettier lawyer anywheres," Murphy said. Again the gallery laughed, and they were quieted this time only by a warning glare from Judge Coit.

"Mr. Murphy," Sue began. "Did you hear any exchange of words between Sheriff Taggert and Mr. Coulter?"

"Naw. It was too noisy inside the saloon. First thing I heard was the shot."

"And you saw nothing?"

"Yeah, I saw something. I seen Taggert come backin' through the doors."

"But, of the actual shooting, you saw nothing?"

"No, that happened out front, on the porch."

"Then you cannot testify as to who drew first, can you?"

"Girly, I didn't have to see it to know who drawed first. I tole you, the gun was still in Taggert's holster."

"Isn't it possible that Mr. Coulter saw Taggert starting for his gun, but drew his own gun so quickly that Taggert was stopped before he could draw?" Sue asked.

Murphy looked at Sue in total surprise. "Are you tryin' to say this here Coutler fella is so fast that he could draw and shoot before Taggert could even clear leather?" He laughed. "That's the most damn fool notion I've ever heard," he said. The gallery laughed with him.

"No further questions, Your Honor," Sue said, her cheeks flaming as she returned to the defense table.

"Redirect, Mr. Foster?"

"No redirect," Foster replied. "Your Honor, despite the obvious inexperience of the defense counsel, I would like to point out that she did bring up one salient point. Neither Mr. Murphy, nor anyone else in the saloon, actually witnessed the shooting. But there is one person who did see the shooting, and that will be my final witness. Prosecution calls to the stand the widow, Mrs. Abby Martindale."

Abby Martindale was a dried up, pinch-faced, perch-mouthed woman. Her hair was combed back into a severe bun, and a pair of rimless glasses rested on the end of her nose. After being sworn, she took her seat in the witness chair. As she waited for the cross-examination to begin, she fidgeted with the dark gray, high-collared dress she was wearing.

Foster got up from his table, and hooking his thumbs in his vest, approached the witness chair. He smiled and nodded, deferentially.

"Now, Mrs. Martindale, I realize that it is a difficult thing to testify in a case like this, and I want you to know how much I appreciate your agreeing to do so."

"I'm only doing my Christian duty," Mrs. Martindale replied self-righteously.

"To be sure," Foster replied. "Now, on the night Sheriff Taggert was murdered . . ."

"Objection, Your Honor," Sue interrupted. "It has not been established that Sheriff Taggert was murdered, only that he was killed."

"Sustained," Coit said.

"Very good, Miss Davenport," Foster said. Looking at her, he clapped his hands slowly and patronizingly. "I'm sure your father, if he were here . . . and sober, would be pleased with you. And you are quite correct, my comment was prejudicial. Therefore, I will rephrase my question." He turned back to the witness. "Now, Mrs. Martindale, on the night Sheriff Taggert was," he paused and looked over toward Sue as he said the next word, setting it apart from the rest of his sentence, ". . . killed . . . were you in your apartment?"

"I was."

"And, what night was that?"

"That would have been Tuesday night, the eighteenth," Mrs. Martindale replied.

"Let the record show that Mrs. Martindale has established the date on which Sheriff Taggert was killed as Tuesday, June the eighteenth," Foster said.

"So ordered," Coit said.

Foster turned back to Mrs. Martindale. "How far is your apartment from the front porch of the Double Eagle?"

"Not very far at all," Mrs. Martindale answered. "My business establishment is just next door to the Double Eagle. Before my husband died, he was half owner of the Double Eagle. After he died, I sold my husband's interest to Mr. Thomas, the current owner of the Double

Eagle, and I used the money to buy the dressmaking and alteration shop I now run."

"Would you say you are close enough to the entrance to be able to hear a conversation that might have taken place on the front porch?"

"Yes, when the window is raised in my apartment, I can easily hear conversations from the front porch of the saloon. In fact, I have overheard some quite shocking things."

"I'll say. You've gotten more than one husband in trouble with that wagging tongue of yours," someone in the gallery shouted, and all laughed. With a stern glare and pounding gavel, Coit restored order.

"On the night of the eighteenth, Mrs. Martindale, did you have cause to raise the window?"

"Yes. As you may recall, it was quite warm that evening," Mrs. Martindale replied.

"Did you hear anything of interest on that night?"

"I heard Sheriff Taggert and another man talking."

"The other man that you overheard, is he now in court?"

"Yes."

"Can you point him out for the court?"

Mrs. Martindale looked over toward the defense table at Win. Then she pointed at him. "That is the man."

"Thank you, Mrs. Martindale. Your Honor, let the record show that Mrs. Martindale has identified the defendant, Win Coulter, as the man she overheard having a conversation with Sheriff Taggert."

"So ordered," Coit replied.

"Was there anything about their conversation that caused—"

"Please the Court, Your Honor, I have Mr. Davenport!" Elam suddenly shouted, interrupting the proceeding as he pushed in, importantly, through the back door.

Chapter 13

"Mr. Davenport, you are late," Coit said.

"I beg your pardon, Your Honor, but I was unavoidably detained."

"More'n likely, he was unavoidably hungover," someone in the courtroom said just under his breath, and the others laughed.

Coit silenced the court with his gavel, then he looked at Dexter. "Are you intoxicated, Mr. Davenport?"

"I am not intoxicated at the moment, Your Honor," Dexter said.

"Approach the bench, please."

Dexter walked down to the front of the courtroom and stood there while Judge Coit looked him over.

"Let me smell your breath," Coit demanded.

"With all due respect, Your Honor, I . . . uh . . . was intoxicated last night and there may be some residual odor. I submit that smelling my breath is not a valid test."

Coit studied Dexter for a long moment. "All right," Coit finally said. "You don't appear to be intoxicated. And due to the court's awareness of your current economic conditions, I will not fine you for contempt for

being late. However, Mr. Davenport, you are put on notice. I will not tolerate any further disregard of this court.
Do you understand?"

"I do, Your Honor."

Coit nodded toward the defendant's table. "You may
take your seat with your client and your co-counsel," he
said.

"Thank you, Your Honor."

"Prosecution may continue."

"Clerk, would you read back my last question,
please?" Foster asked.

The clerk read in a monotone voice: "Was there anything about their conversation that caused. . . . and that
is as far as you got."

"Thank you. Mrs. Martindale, was there anything in
their conversation that caused you to pay particular attention to what they were saying?"

"I don't understand the question."

"Were their words loud or angry?"

"Loud? Angry? No," Mrs. Martindale replied, "but
they were frightening."

"They weren't loud or angry, but they were frightening? How so?"

"The words were cold and calculating," Mrs. Martindale said.

"Cold and calculating. Would you say they were killing words?"

"Objection," Dexter called out. "Prosecution is leading the witness."

"Sustained."

"All right, I'll strike that. We'll go with cold, calculating, and frightening. Did there seem to be a disagreement between them?"

"Yes," Mrs. Martindale said.

"And what was the disagreement about?"

"Evidently Mr. Coulter wanted to go into the saloon,
but the sheriff was opposed to that."

"What makes you think that?"

"I heard the sheriff say, 'Mister, I told you, you ain't comin' in here and that's just the way it's goin' to be.' "

"How did Coulter respond?"

"He didn't say anything," Mrs. Martindale said. "So the sheriff spoke again. 'Time's runnin' short,' the sheriff said. 'What are you goin' to do?' "

"Was there a reply to that?" Foster asked.

"Yes. Mr. Coulter said, 'I'm going to do just what I told you I was going to do. I'm going in there to get myself some supper and a couple of beers. Now, you can either step aside and let me by, or stay where you are while I come through you.' "

Foster turned toward the jury and held his finger up. "Step aside and let me by, or stay where you are while I come through you," he said. He turned back to Mrs. Martindale. "What was said next?"

"Nothing was said next," Mrs. Martindale replied.

"Nothing? You mean nothing else happened?"

Mrs. Martindale shook her head. "I didn't say that. I said no more words were spoken. The next thing I knew, there was a gun in Mr. Coulter's hand. I saw the flash and heard the sound of the shot."

"Then what?"

"Then Mr. Coulter passed out of my view, going into the saloon."

"Now, Mrs. Martindale, and this is very important," Foster said. "Did you see who drew first?"

"Yes."

"And, who drew first?"

"Mr. Coulter drew first," she said. "One moment there was nothing in his hand, and the next moment . . . almost as quick as thought, he was holding, and shooting his gun."

"Thank you," Foster said. He looked over at the defense table. "Your witness, Mr. Davenport."

Dexter got up from the defense table and walked over to Mrs. Martindale.

"Mrs. Martindale, did you see Sheriff Taggert start to draw?"

"No."

"You didn't see him draw, because in fact, you didn't see him at all. Is that correct?"

"Objection! It has already been established that Mrs. Martindale was a witness through her window that night!"

"I submit, Your Honor, that Mrs. Martindale was a witness to only one-half of the drama. One of the reasons I was late this morning, is because I asked Mrs. Martindale's maid to allow me into her apartment so I could examine the window through which she witnessed the shooting. In doing so, I discovered an interesting fact. From the chair Mrs. Martindale occupies during her window eavesdrops, her view of the front of the saloon is limited. She can see the front steps to the porch, but, because of the porch roof, a significant part of the porch is blocked from her view." Dexter then turned his attention back to the witness. "You heard them both speaking that night, but, you didn't actually see Sheriff Taggert. That's true, isn't it, Mrs. Martindale?"

"Well, yes, if you mean did I actually see the sheriff, then the answer is no. He wasn't in my direct view."

"That being the case, it is very possible that Sheriff Taggert started his draw before Mr. Coulter, but you didn't see it."

Mrs. Martindale shook her head. "Based on what I was seeing and overhearing, I just don't think that is the way it happened. I stand by my statement that Mr. Coulter drew first."

"I see," Dexter said. He started back toward his table then he stopped and looked back at her. "Mrs. Martindale, you didn't actually see Mr. Coulter start his draw either, did you?"

"I beg your pardon?"

Dexter closed the rest of the distance to his table, then read from his notes, "You said, and I quote, 'One moment there was nothing in his hand, and the next moment . . . almost as quick as thought, he was holding and shooting his gun.' By your own account Mrs. Martindale, Mr. Coulter was so fast, that you didn't see him start his draw. You saw only the conclusion . . . when the gun was actually in his hand. But a conclusion must have a beginning. He obviously started his draw, even though you didn't see it. Isn't that correct?"

"Yes . . . I . . . I suppose that is so," Mrs. Martindale agreed.

"So then, if you didn't see either man begin their draw, it is impossible for you to say who drew first."

"I . . . I guess so."

"Thus, Mr. Coulter's statement that Sheriff Taggert drew first remains unchallenged by any eyewitness," Dexter said triumphantly to the jury. He turned back toward Mrs. Martindale, who was still sitting in the witness chair. A look of confusion had replaced what had been an expression of smug correctness.

"Thank you, Mrs. Martindale. No further questions," Dexter said as he sat down. Smiling in support, Sue put her hand on her father's arm.

"Redirect, Mr. Foster?" Coit asked.

Foster stood, but he didn't leave his table. "Mrs. Martindale, before the incident the other night, did you ever have occasion to see Sheriff Taggert use his gun?"

"Yes, when my husband was alive and running the saloon. I was witness to a gunfight between Sheriff Taggert, Lee Trevett, and Angus Pugh."

"Yes, I remember that. In fact, you gave testimony in court in regard to that shooting, did you not?"

"I did."

"On that occasion, by his speed and skill with a pistol,

Sheriff Taggert prevailed over not one, but two would-be assassins?"

"Yes."

"So, even if, as defense claims, you were unable to see Sheriff Taggert on the night of the eighteenth, you have in fact seen him in action before."

"Yes, I have."

"Now, on the night of the eighteenth, you saw Mr. Coulter, which means you have seen both men under similar conditions. Based upon your observation, which of the two do you think is the faster?"

"Objection!" Dexter said. "You Honor, you can't ask a person to make a comparison based upon seeing one person draw at one time and another at another time. She would have to see both of them at the same time!"

"Your Honor, I'm not really asking the witness to make a comparison in the sense Mr. Davenport is thinking. She has already testified that she believed Coulter drew first. I am just providing her with the empirical evidence that will allow her to substantiate the belief she has already stated."

"Defense objection is overruled," Coit said.

"Exception! To allow such convoluted logic would be a gross miscarriage of justice," Dexter shouted.

"Be very, very careful with me, Mr. Davenport," Judge Coit warned, shaking his finger at him. "I have said I will allow Mr. Foster's argument to stand and that's it."

"Thank you, Your Honor," Foster said. "I have no more questions."

Chapter 14

BEN ANDERS CLIMBED UP ONTO A ROCK FROM WHICH he could see for nearly two miles back across the desert. A small rise hid everything beyond that point.

"See anything?" Moe Jacoby asked.

"No," Anders answered.

Jacoby, a short, hairy man with gray eyes and a pug nose took the last swallow from a whiskey bottle, then tossed it against a nearby rock. The bottle broke into two pieces.

"Goddammit, Jacoby, what for'd you break that bottle?" Anders asked, looking around at him. "We could'a got us five cents for it back in town."

"Five cents," Jacoby snorted. "If you'd sell that gold tooth of your'n, you get a lot more than five cents."

"I ain't goin' to sell my gold tooth. If you're so all-fired anxious to sell somethin', we could sell that watch you got."

"You keep your hands off my watch. Anyhow, the deal we got goin' now is goin' to bring us enough money than your gold tooth or my watch," Jacoby said.

"Yeah, well, I ain't seen no money yet."

"All we have to do is take care of the Coulters, and

we'll get our share," Jacoby insisted. "Now, look again."

"We ain't got Win Coulter to worry about now. He'll be hung before nightfall."

"Don't count your chickens before they hatch," Jacoby cautioned. "When you shot his horse, you thought the son of a bitch would die on the desert, but he didn't. You should'a killed him when you had the chance."

"Who would'a thought he would make as far as he did?" Anders replied. "Anyway, the judge'll take care of him."

"That leaves Joe Coulter for us."

"Maybe he ain't comin'," Anders said.

"He's comin'," Jacoby said. "I can feel it in my gut. He is out there, and he's close."

Anders climbed down from the rock and walked over to his horse. He slipped his rifle out of the saddle holster.

"What are you fixin' to do?" Jacoby asked.

"If he's really comin', like you say he is, I don't aim to let him get any closer'n a rifle shot."

"Yeah," Jacoby agreed. "Yeah, that's a good idea. We'll just shoot the son of a bitch down, soon as he comes into range."

The two men, with rifles in hand, climbed back up onto the rock which afforded them, not only a good view of the approaching trail, but also some cover and concealment. They checked the loads in their rifles, eased the hammers back to half-cock, then hunkered down on the rock and waited.

"Let 'im come up to no more'n about a hundred yards," Jacoby suggested. "We got all the advantage. He don't have any idea we're here."

"I still say he ain't comin'," Anders said.

At that moment, a rider came into view over a distant rise.

"He ain't, huh?" Jacoby said with the smug air of "I told you so." "Then who is that?"

"Son of a bitch! It's him!" Anders said. He raised his rifle to his shoulder.

"Hold it!" Jacoby said, reaching out to pull the rifle back down. "Be patient. You shoot now, you won't do no more'n spook him. Let him get close, like I said."

"All right," Anders said, nervously.

They waited as the distant rider came closer, sometimes seeming not to be riding, but rather floating as he materialized and dematerialized in the heat waves that were rising from the desert floor.

On he came, to a mile, half a mile, a quarter mile. Jacoby raised his rifle and rested it carefully against the rock, taking a very careful aim. "Just a little closer," he said, quietly. "A little closer before we fire."

Anders shifted position to get a better aim. As he did so he dislodged a loose stone, and the stone rolled down the rock, right into the largest, unbroken piece of the whiskey bottle. The stone shattered the glass and it made a loud, tinkling noise.

"Goddammit!" Jacoby shouted angrily. "You dumb bastard, you just gave away our position!" He raised up and fired his first shot.

The sound of the crashing bottle reached Joe Coulter's ears at about the same time Jacoby reared up to fire. Joe could see that ahead, on the trail, a man was holding a rifle pointed at him.

"What the hell?" he shouted, pulling his pistol at the same time. He snapped off a shot, knowing he was out of range, hoping only to make the ambusher hurry his own shot. The ploy worked. Jacoby fired quickly, then dropped back down behind the rock.

Joe slid down from his horse quickly, slipping his rifle from the holster as he did so. Slapping his horse to get him out of the line of fire, he ran, bending over, toward a nearby rock formation. Two shots whined off the rocks just as he got behind them. The shots were so close together that, even though he had only seen one man, he knew that there were at least two of them laying for him.

Joe raised up and fired his rifle toward the place where the shots had come from, even though he didn't have a target. Looking around, he saw a dry creek bed. If he could make it there, he could work his way up closer to the ambushers without coming under their fire.

"Anders, you dumb son of a bitch!" Jacoby swore. "Iffen you hadn't kicked that rock down we would'a had him by now."

"Hell, I'm not the one put the bottle there," Anders said. "Where is he, anyhow?" Anders stuck his head cautiously over the rock and looked down where the target had been. "Where is he? I can't see him."

"I don't know," Jacoby admitted. "I saw him get behind that rock, but I ain't seen him since."

"There's a dry creek bed down there. I seen it when we come through," Anders said.

Jacoby looked toward him. "A dry creek bed? Damn, he could be right on us before we even knew it."

Anders shook his head. "I don't think so," he said. "It curves away a long time before it gets up here."

No sooner were the words out of Anders' mouth than there was a puff of smoke and the bark of a rifle from a clump of bushes not too far distant. The bullet hit the rock right in front of them, then hummed off, but not before shaving off a sliver of lead to kick up into Anders' face.

"Ow! I been hit, I been hit!" Anders called, slapping his hand to his face. "I been shot right in the jaw!"

Jacoby looked at him, then laughed.

"What do you think is so goddamned funny?" Anders complained.

"You are. You are funny," Jacoby said. "You ain't been hit. That ain't nothin' but a shaving."

Two more bullets hit the rocks then and chips of stone flew past them.

"I don't like this," Jacoby said. "He's gettin' too damn close." Jacoby fired a couple of shots toward the bush just below the puff of gun smoke.

"Hey, Jacoby, look down there," Anders said. "Ain't that his horse comin' back up the road?"

"Yeah," Jacoby said. He giggled. "This is great! Shoot the horse! We'll just leave the son of a bitch out here to die."

"That didn't work the other time. What makes you think it'll work this time?" Anders asked.

"Do you have a better idea?" Jacoby challenged.

"No," Anders admitted.

"Then shoot the goddamned horse."

Both men started shooting at the horse, but the animal was still a couple of hundred yards away and slightly downhill. As a result, it wasn't hit, though the bullets striking the ground nearby caused the horse to turn and run toward the shelter of a bluff, a quarter of a mile away.

"Dammit! We missed!" Jacoby said.

Another bullet hit the rock, very close beside them.

"Let's get the hell out of here!" Anders shouted. He started running for his own horse.

"Anders! Come back here!" Jacoby called, chasing after him.

Seeing the two men start to run, Joe tracked them with his rifle, firing at the man in the lead. That man went down, but the other made it to his horse. He kicked his horse into motion and in just a few seconds was behind a rocky ledge, out of the line of fire.

"Don't leave me, you bastard!" the one on the ground shouted. "Don't you leave me!"

Joe approached the man on the ground, holding his weapon pointed toward him. Seeing him, the man sat up and threw up his hands. "Don't shoot, don't shoot," he begged. "I'm hurt. I'm hurt bad."

"Your name is Anders?" Joe asked, when he reached the wounded man.

Anders looked surprised. "How do you know my name?"

"You two boys weren't exactly keepin' secrets," Joe said. "I heard the other man call your name. Why did you ambush me?"

"You got to get me to the doctor," Anders said, without answering Joe's question. "If this wound ain't treated, I could wind up losin' my leg."

"That's right, you could," Joe said laconically. Putting his rifle down, he knelt beside Anders. He cut the trouser leg away with his knife and saw the ugly black hole where the rifle bullet had gone into the flesh. The bullet had come out the other side. There was a good amount of blood, but it wasn't pumping as it would have been had an artery been hit. And there didn't appear to be any shattered bone. Joe ripped up some more of Anders' trouser leg and used it to make a bandage, tying it in place with strips of cloth.

"You aren't hurt all that bad," he said.

"The hell I ain't. What do you know about it, anyway?"

"I've treated gunshot wounds before."

"Yeah, well, you ain't ever treated one of mine."

"The one who got away," Joe said. "What was his name?"

"Why the hell should I tell you that?"

Joe pulled his gun and put the barrel of his pistol to Anders' forehead.

"Because I will shoot you if you don't."

"You're bluffing."

Joe cocked his pistol. "When you get to hell, say hello to Quantrill for me," he said, matter-of-factly. His finger twitched on the trigger.

"No, wait!" Anders screamed as he pissed in his pants. "His name is Jacoby. Moe Jacoby!"

Joe eased the hammer down on his pistol. "Now, Anders, why are you trying to kill us?"

"Why does anyone do anything? For money," Anders explained. He was still shaking with fear.

"Money? Where are you going to get money from killing us? There's no paper out on us out here. How do you expect to collect a reward?" Joe asked.

"A reward? Who's looking for a reward?" Anders asked.

Joe was confused. "You said you were trying to kill us for money. If there's no reward, where is the money coming from?"

"Are you kidding?" Anders replied. "Hell, you should know better'n anyone where the money is coming from."

Joe had no idea what Anders was talking about, but he decided to let it drop for the moment. Instead, he went over to Anders' horse and started to mount.

"Hey, wait a minute! What are you doin'? You're stealin' my horse," Anders asked.

"I'm just borrowing it to ride down to collect mine," Joe said. "I'll be back in a minute or two."

"How do I know you will be back? You could be lyin', plannin' to leave me out here."

"I could be," Joe said, easily.

Joe rode down to where his own horse stood, quietly waiting. He got off Anders' horse and mounted his own, then returned, leading the animal he had borrowed.

"You come back. I didn't figure you'd come back," Anders said.

"Get on," Joe ordered. "We're going into Horseshoe."

Anders mounted with some effort, though Joe was of the opinion that Anders was letting on as if he was hurting much more than he was.

Joe's opinion was right. Anders was playing for time,

looking for the right moment. When Joe turned away from him, Anders figured that the right moment had arrived. He pulled a hidden pistol from his bedroll and fired at Joe.

Until that moment, Anders' plan had gone well. He had caught Joe by surprise, pulling and firing his pistol before Joe even realized that a second gun existed. But he missed, and that was his error. His fatal error, as it turned out, because even as Anders' bullet was whizzing by Joe's head, Joe was already turning, his pistol blazing in his hand.

Joe's bullet caught Anders in the chest, knocking him from his horse and killing him before he even hit the ground.

Joe rode over to Anders' body and looked down at it. He gave a passing thought to burying him, then shrugged. Let the buzzards have the bastard.

Chapter 15

"A DEMONSTRATION?" COIT ASKED. "WHAT SORT OF demonstration?"

"A demonstration of my client's expertise with the pistol, Your Honor," Dexter said.

"Let me see if I understand this. You are asking me to put a weapon in the hand of your client . . . put a gun in the hand of a known killer, so he can give us a demonstration of his skills with that instrument?"

"Yes, Your Honor," Dexter replied.

"What makes you think I would even consider such a ridiculous request?"

"Because, Your Honor, my entire case depends upon it," Dexter said. "Prosecution claims that Mr. Coulter drew first. He had to draw first, prosecution argues, because no man alive is fast enough to have beaten Sheriff Taggert. But it is our contention that Mr. Coulter is fast enough to have done that very thing."

"Your Honor, what would a demonstration accomplish?" Foster asked. "If the court watches him pull a pistol from his holster, we might all agree that he is fast, perhaps faster than anyone any of us have seen. But it would prove nothing, because he would be drawing alone. There would be no standard by which we could make our assessment."

"You have a point, counselor," Judge Coit agreed.

"Your Honor, we have considered that very thing," Dexter said. "In fact, that is the point I tried to make when I suggested that Mrs. Martindale could not judge the relative speed of the two men, based upon watching them perform individually. But, I believe we have crafted a demonstration that would accommodate that concern."

"What sort of demonstration would that be?" Coit asked.

"It is a demonstration suggested by my client," Dexter replied. He walked back over to the table and picked up a pie pan and a silver dollar. He put the pie pan, upside down, on the floor. The gallery buzzed in curiosity.

"What's the pan for?" someone asked.

"What's he aimin' to do?" another questioned.

"This is how the demonstration will work," Dexter explained. He stuck his hand out in front of him. "My client will hold his hand straight out in front of him, like so, palm down." With his other hand, Dexter held up the silver dollar. "This coin will rest on the back of his hand, like this." Dexter put the coin on the back of his hand so that he was now holding it out in front of him. "When he turns his hand to start for his gun, the silver dollar will fall toward the pie plate. Mr. Coulter will then draw his pistol and shoot two times, hitting his target both times before the silver coin strikes the pie plate."

Dexter turned his hand. Then, even though he wasn't wearing a gun and holster, he acted as if he were drawing and shooting a pistol. Pointedly, the coin clanked against the pan before Dexter could even raise his hand back up from the imaginary holster. The gallery laughed at his failure.

"Why, that's impossible," Coit said. "You couldn't

even do it without a gun . . . let alone actually draw and shoot."

"That is true, Your Honor, I couldn't, and I daresay there are few who could. Therefore, such an exhibition, if successfully performed, would clearly demonstrate my client's speed and skill with a pistol, would it not?" Dexter asked.

"Mr. Coulter," Coit asked, leaning over his desk and looking over toward the defense table. "Can you actually do such a thing?"

"I think I can," Win replied.

"You *think* you can?" Coit repeated.

"I'm pretty sure I can."

"I think I'd like to see that."

"Your Honor, I strenuously object!" Foster said. "I could see allowing him to make a demonstration with an empty pistol. But what you propose now, is giving him a loaded gun. Do you understand the gravity of this? You are actually going to let him have bullets in that gun!"

"Mr. Foster, you are the one who said that a demonstration with an unloaded pistol would be a waste of time," Coit reminded him.

"Yes, but . . . to give an accused murderer a loaded gun?"

"The court will take every precaution," Judge Coit promised. "Deputy Elam."

"Yes, Your Honor?"

"While the demonstration is in progress, you will stand nearby. At all times, your pistol will be drawn, and aimed at Mr. Coulter. If he deviates one iota from the script as outlined by Mr. Davenport, you will shoot him."

Elam smiled broadly. "Yes, sir, Your Honor, it will be my pleasure," he said.

"This court will take a five-minute recess," Coit said. "At the conclusion of that five minutes, we will reconvene out on the street in front. At that time, and in that place, Mr. Coulter will demonstrate his prowess as a marksman."

Coit rapped on the table, then got up and retired quickly. When he was gone, the rest of the court stood, then started toward the back door, buzzing in excitement over the unexpected entertainment.

Outside of the courthouse the finishing touches were being put on the gallows. The judge had already made it clear that not only did he intend to find Win guilty today, he intended to hang him today as well.

"Mr. Coulter, I have to tell you that I am worried about this," Sue said as she, Win, and her father walked out under the watchful eye of Deputy Elam.

"What is there to worry about?" Win asked.

"If you stop and think about it, this is a loaded situation. Even if you can do what you say, we will still have to make a case for self-defense. But if you *can't* do it, the prosecution will be able to claim that their case is already made."

"I'm afraid my daughter might be right," Dexter said. "I'm now beginning to wish that I had not listened to you when you came up with this idea."

"The problem is the bell has been rung and we can't un-ring it," Sue said. "If you back out now, it's the same as admitting defeat."

"Then, I'll just have to do it, won't I?" Win said.

By now, the entire court had reassembled in the street in front of the courthouse, to include the judge, clerk, and jury. A paper target was put on a wagon, and the wagon was pulled away, approximately fifty feet.

"Your Honor, I object," Dexter said, when he saw the position of the wagon. "At the time of the actual shooting, the two belligerents were no more than ten feet apart. You've put this target much too far away."

"I've put it there for the safety of the observers," Coit

said. "I can't see that its location should make that much difference."

"Hell, it would for me," someone in the crowd said. "I doubt if I could even hit the wagon from here, let alone that little target."

The others laughed, but Judge Coit's fixed glare forestalled any additional comments.

"Johnson?" the judge said to one of the men in the crowd.

"Yes, sir?" Johnson replied.

"Take all the bullets but two from your gun, then hand your pistol and belt over to the defendant."

"Your Honor, I ask that the defendant be allowed to use his own gun and holster," Dexter said. "After all, this is no small feat we are asking of him."

"Where is his gun and holster?" Coit asked. "I will not hold the proceedings up any longer while you send someone for it."

"I have it with me, Your Honor," Sue said. Reaching into her oversized reticule, she pulled out Win's holster and pistol, tied up with its own belt.

"Bring it to me," Coit instructed.

Sue handed it to him. The judge checked the cylinders and, satisfied that only two chambers were charged, handed it back to Sue. "Deputy Elam," Coit said. "Draw your pistol and point it at the defendant."

Elam drew his gun and pointed it at Win.

"Now, Miss Davenport, you may give Mr. Coulter his pistol."

Sue handed the gun and holster to Win. Win smiled at her, then strapped the rig on. He loosened the gun in his holster, a couple of times, then nodded at Dexter. Dexter put the pie pan on the ground in front of him, then handed Win the silver dollar. Win stretched out his hand and put the coin on the back of his hand.

"Are you ready, Mr. Coulter?" Judge Coit said.

"Wait, I can't do it like this," Win said.

The crowd buzzed at Win's answer.

"I knew he couldn't do it," someone said.

"Hell, no man could," another added.

"Then, I take it you are ready to admit defeat?" Coit asked.

"No, that's not what I meant," Win answered. He was still holding his hand out in front of him. "I meant that in order to do this I need an element of danger. Nothing makes a gunman faster than the thought that if he doesn't succeed, he'll be killed."

"Do you have a proposal as to how we may add that element of danger?" Coit asked.

"I do," Win answered with a smile. He looked over at the deputy, who was still pointing his pistol at Win. "Elam, if I don't pull my gun and shoot the target before you hear the coin hit the pie pan, I want you to shoot me."

"What?" Sue asked. Her incredulous response was met with a buzz of excitement and disbelief from those in the crowd.

"Mister, you gone plumb loco? Elam would like nothing more than to shoot you," someone said.

"Yeah, and how do you know he won't start shooting even before he hears the coin clank?" another asked.

"What'll I do, Judge?" Elam asked, unsure of himself.

"You heard the man, Deputy," Coit replied. "If he doesn't get his two shots off before the coin hits the pie pan, shoot him."

Elam smiled broadly. "Yes, *sir*, Your Honor. I'll do that gladly!"

"Win! Have you gone crazy?" Sue asked in alarm.

Win looked over at her and winked.

"Alright, ever'one back out of the way," Coit said. "Mr. Coulter, anytime you're ready."

At the time everyone started filing out of the court-room, the carpenters were still working on the gallows. But word spread quickly as to what was about to happen, so the carpenters abandoned their saws and hammers and came down to watch. At the same time, drinkers left the saloon, clerks and customers quit the stores, men came from the livery and the freight company, housewives abandoned their washing, and children ran from the school to see the show. Like ants swarming to a sugar cube, the crowd in front of the courthouse swelled to well over two hundred people. In fact, the only citizens of the town who weren't present, were those few who were too sick, too old, or too young. And now, as they waited for the demonstration, the whispered buzz of excitement stilled, and the crowd became absolutely silent.

A sign squeaked in the wind.

Time itself, waited.

Then, suddenly, Win turned his hand, and the crowd drew a collective breath as the coin started falling toward the pie pan. In the blink of an eye, the gun was in Win's hand. It cracked once . . . twice . . . then the coin hit the pan. It was all over before the crowd realized that Win's first shot had not been at the target, but at the gun in Elam's hand. It was not until Elam shouted out in pain and anger that everyone realized what happened.

"You . . . you son of a bitch, you shot me!" Elam shouted, holding his hand. A trickle of blood was running down from his middle finger. It had been creased just enough to make him drop the gun, though the finger had not been crushed by the impact of the bullet.

"He hit the target dead center," someone called from down by the wagon. That had been Win's second shot.

There was a spontaneous burst of applause, silenced only when Judge Coit was able to regain control.

"Deputy, retrieve your pistol," Coit said.

Grumbling, Elam did as the judge asked.

"Now, if you would, please escort the prisoner back into the court."

Chapter 16

As the court members and gallery filed back into the community building, they were still expressing awe and disbelief over what they had just witnessed.

"In all my borned days, I ain't never seen nothin' like that."

"I didn't think it was humanly possible for anyone to be that fast."

"Sheriff Taggert was fast, but he wasn't nowhere near to being that fast."

Even the members of the jury, men who were supposed to be impartial witnesses, expressed their amazement over what they had just seen.

Judge Coit called the court back to order, then directed that the trial continue. Dexter Davenport was invited to give his summation.

"Gentlemen of the jury, the law is very clear," Dexter began. "In order to bring a verdict of guilty, you must establish a trinity of events. You must establish that Coulter had the opportunity to kill Taggert . . . that he had the means to kill Taggert . . . and finally, the motive to kill Taggert.

"You heard Mrs. Martindale testify that Coulter and

Taggert stood face to face on the front porch of The Double Eagle saloon. Defense will stipulate, therefore, that this did present Coulter with the opportunity to kill Taggert. But I ask you to remember this. Coulter's horse was killed out in the middle of the desert, and he was forced to walk nearly twenty miles in blistering heat . . . without water . . . to get here. I submit to you therefore, that this was an opportunity born of fate, not of afore-thought. You are trying a case of first degree murder. And, without malice and aforethought, *there . . . can . . . be . . . no . . . conviction.*

"Secondly, we must consider if he had the means to kill Sheriff Taggert. Defense will also stipulate that yes, Mr. Coulter did have the means. In fact, we just wit-nessed a remarkable demonstration in which Mr. Coulter proved to us that he had the means to best Taggert in a gunfight, even if Taggert drew first. If Taggert drew first, *there . . . can . . . be . . . no . . . conviction.*

"It is Mr. Coulter's contention that Taggert did draw first, and we have no direct eyewitnesses who can testify to the contrary."

Here, Dexter paused and stared hard at each member of the jury, all of whom were sitting spellbound by his oratory. "If there is the slightest chance that Coulter might be telling the truth . . . then that alone is sufficient to cast a shadow of doubt over his guilt. Remember that, because if there is the slightest doubt, *there . . . can . . . be . . . no . . . conviction.*

"And now, to the third branch of our trinity. We have discussed opportunity and means. Let us now discuss motive. All three elements must be considered in bring-ing about a guilty verdict. And, while we will stipulate as to opportunity and means, the lack of motive is glar-ing. What was Win Coulter's motive? Why would he have walked twenty miles across a barren desert just to kill Sheriff Taggert?

"The answer is, he wouldn't have. The only reason he

killed Sheriff Taggert, was because Sheriff Taggert was trying to kill him. And that isn't motive, that is self-defense. And if Coulter acted in self-defense, *there . . . can . . . be . . . no . . . conviction.*"

As in each of the previous times, Dexter set the words of his mantra apart, allowing them to sink in. After an extended silence, he resumed his summation.

"And finally, before you render your verdict, I ask each and every one of you to look deep into your inner souls. Consider all that I have told you. The burden of proof is upon the prosecution. If there is the slightest chance that you believe Mr. Coulter's story . . . that you believe he was braced on the front porch of The Double Eagle saloon . . . and that he did not draw his gun until he perceived his life to be in mortal danger, then *there . . . can . . . be . . . no . . . conviction.*

"Thank you."

Sue was smiling proudly at her father as he returned to his chair behind the table for the defense. Win leaned over to him.

"You've done a good job for me, Mr. Davenport," he said. "Regardless of how this comes out, I couldn't have asked for a better lawyer."

"Thank you, my boy," Dexter said. His eyes were misted over with tears. "Odd, how things work out, isn't it? I am trying hard to save your life, and in so doing, I may have just saved my own."

"Prosecution, your closing remarks?" Judge Coit invited.

Standing, Brigham Foster looked over toward the defense table. "Before I address this court, Your Honor, let me first congratulate Mr. Davenport on the fine and spirited defense he has put up for Win Coulter. To those of us who have grown accustomed to seeing him drunk, it is heartening to see him sober."

"That was a backhanded compliment if I have ever heard one," Sue said under her breath.

"I don't think it was a compliment, dear," Dexter replied. "Wait for the other shoe to drop. Mr. Foster is far too calculating for empty compliments."

Foster approached the jury.

"Some of you may have wondered how a man of Dexter Davenport's obvious intelligence and talent could have fallen so far.

"To answer that question, we must go back to a trial that took place in this very building, two years ago. At that trial our positions were reversed. Davenport, until then, a fine, upstanding lawyer and leading citizen of Horseshoe, was prosecuting. I, the younger and more inexperienced lawyer, was defending.

"The defendants were Sheriff Taggert and Moe Jacoby. You see, gentlemen of the jury, Sue Davenport thought Luke Taggert would make a fine husband, so, she threw herself at him, only to have him reject her. And, as the saying goes, hell hath no fury like a woman scorned.

"Sue Davenport then took revenge upon the sheriff by accusing him of raping her. But, her fury was so great that she didn't stop with Taggert. He accusation took in Mr. Jacoby as well. Now, rape is a foul crime, and society is justifiably harsh with the perpetrators of such an act. But, because of that very harshness, we must also be certain that the accusation is true. Alas, the charges brought against Sheriff Taggert and Mr. Jacoby by Sue Davenport were proven, in this very court, and with this very judge," Foster pointed to Coit, "to be false. Luke Taggert and Moe Jacoby were exonerated.

"Dexter Davenport had fought hard to uphold the honor of his daughter, but he was fighting an uphill battle, because truth has a way of winning out over even the cleverest and most skilled lawyer. Unable to face the humiliation his daughter had brought down upon them, Dexter Davenport took to drink. The result of his failing battle with demon rum is the poor wretch we all know today.

"You may be wondering, gentlemen of the jury, why I told you this story. I told it, not to further embarrass Mr. Davenport, but to supply you with that missing element in the trinity that the defense counsel so clearly laid out for us. If you will recall, Mr. Davenport stipulated as to means and opportunity. But where, he asked, was the motive?

"The motive, gentlemen, is right here."

Dramatically, Foster pointed to Sue Davenport.

"Win Coulter killed Sheriff Taggert to avenge this vindictive woman."

"What?" Sue shouted out loud.

"Objection!" Dexter yelled.

Coit banged his gavel.

"Mr. Davenport, Miss Davenport, silence during summation."

"Your Honor, this isn't summation, this is a new charge. None of the information the prosecutor spoke of was introduced during the trial." Dexter looked at Foster. "Are you accusing my daughter of hiring this man to kill Sheriff Taggert?"

"No, not at all," Foster said quickly. "Indeed, I am positive she is innocent of it. I contend that Coulter did it on his own, without the prior consent of Sue Davenport, perhaps in hopes of winning her favor. She is, after all, a very beautiful young woman."

"Your Honor, this is preposterous!" Dexter said. "Neither my daughter nor I had ever met, nor even heard of Mr. Coulter before this trial began."

Foster looked at the men in the jury. "Is it preposterous, gentlemen? Suppose I told you that on the very next day after Sheriff Taggert was killed . . . Sue Davenport was seen kissing Win Coulter through the bars of his jail cell by none other than Judge Coit himself?"

"That's true," Coit said. "I did see them kissing."

After the reaction from the gallery, Foster continued his summation. "Despite Miss Davenport's questionable background, I don't think anyone is ready to believe that she is a woman of such loose morals that she would kiss a man whom she met for the first time."

"My daughter is not a woman of loose morals, and you know that!" Dexter shouted in anger.

"Indeed, I do know that, sir," Foster replied, almost patronizingly. "That is why I submit that there had to be some earlier collusion . . . either inferred by your daughter . . . or imagined by Win Coulter. I am willing to believe that it was imagined by Win Coulter. But in any case, it does provide the motive you so ardently suggested was missing. And in so doing, satisfies the requirements for the jury to find a verdict of guilty of first degree murder." Foster turned back toward the jury. "And with that, gentlemen of the jury, I rest my case."

Brigham Foster's fiery and scathing accusation, stunned the gallery, and they sat in absolute silence as Foster returned to his seat.

Judge Coit began his instructions.

"You have heard the case as presented by both defense and prosecution. It is not necessary for you to consider who killed Sheriff Taggert, for that issue is not in contention. Clearly, Sheriff Taggert was killed by Win Coulter. The only thing you must decide is whether this killing was murder, or self-defense.

"If, somehow, you can overcome the clear evidence that Sheriff Foster's gun was still in his holster when he died, and actually believe he drew first, then it is self-defense, and you must acquit.

"On the other hand, if you think that the fact that Sheriff Taggert's gun was still in its holster is compelling physical evidence that he couldn't have started his draw, it is murder, and you must convict.

"The first consideration, it seems to me, requires a suspension of belief. The second consideration requires merely the acceptance of the preponderance of evidence.

"You may now retire to consider the verdict."

"My God!" Dexter said under his breath. "Coit has just all but ordered the jury to return a verdict of guilty."

The jury met in the farthest corner of the room to deliberate. Deputy Elam stood guard to keep away the many people who wanted to offer their own suggestions. In the meantime, Win, Dexter, and Sue waited at the defense table.

"I want to apologize to you, Mr. Coulter, for having your name dragged through my own, personal slime and mud," Dexter said.

"I don't think anyone will actually believe Foster's claim that there is a connection," Win said.

"On the contrary," Dexter said. "There is an element of truth in what he said. When Taggert and Jacoby . . . ," he looked at Sue, then paused. Sue reached across the table to put her hand on his.

"You can say it, Pa," she said. "When they raped me."

Dexter nodded. "When those two monsters raped my daughter, they thought they could get away with it because they were representatives of the law. I, on the other hand, was a pompous, arrogant fool. I was absolutely positive that the law they proposed to uphold, the very law that I revered, would turn upon those despoilers of the sacred trust and take care of them."

"That's the trial Foster was talking about?" Win asked.

"Yes," Dexter said. "I lost the case, and Taggert and Jacoby went free. I failed my own daughter when she needed me most." Dexter hung his head in shame, and a tear began to slide down his cheek.

"You didn't fail me, Pa. The jury was frightened of them," Sue said. "We never had a chance with the jury."

"I'm talking about after the trial," Dexter said, and he put his other hand on top of Sue's to squeeze it. "I failed

you when I started drinking. I've no excuse for the way
I have behaved these past two years. When you needed
me most is when I was at my worst. I can only beg you
to forgive me . . . and promise you that, beginning now,
I am going to make every effort to regain my life . . .
and my dignity."

Father and daughter were in the midst of an embrace
when someone called out.

"The jury is coming back!"

Win looked toward the corner of the room where the
jury had been meeting and saw that the twelve men were
returning to the area that had been set aside as the jury
box.

"Order in the court!" the clerk shouted, and the mill-
ing, buzzing throng of people quickly took their seats to
see what verdict the jury would deliver.

"Defendant will rise," Coit said.

Win stood.

"Face the jury."

Win turned toward the jury.

"Gentlemen of the jury, have you reached a verdict?"
Coit asked.

"Yeah, we have."

Coit glared at the foreman of the jury.

"You will address this court with respect," Coit demanded.

"Oh, uh, yeah, I mean, yes, sir . . . uh . . . yes, Your
Honor."

"Publish the verdict, please."

"What?" the foreman asked, confused by the term.

"Please tell the court your verdict."

"Well, by a vote of nine to three, we find the defendant not guilty."

The gallery reaction was immediate as dozens of
voices sounded.

"Damn, Dexter, you done it!" someone from the gallery shouted.

"No," Dexter said, speaking under his breath. He was shaking his head. "This isn't right. There's something wrong here."

The loudest voice of all was coming from Foster. He continued to shout until Win was able to hear what he was saying.

"Objection, Your Honor, objection! The verdict must be unanimous!"

"Is that right?" Win asked. "Does it have to be unanimous?"

"I'm afraid so."

"Your Honor, I call for a mistrial!" Foster shouted.

"What does that mean? A mistrial?" Win asked.

"It means we have to do this all over."

Coit began banging his gavel, and he continued to bang it until the courtroom was absolutely quiet. When you could hear a pin drop, he looked over toward the jury.

"Is there any chance of the twelve of you coming up with a unanimous verdict?"

The foreman shook his head. "There ain't a chance in hell, Judge. They's nine of 'em says he ain't guilty, and they ain't goin' to change their minds, no matter what we say to 'em." The foreman then looked over at Win. "But then, they's three of us says Coulter is guilty as hell, and we want to see the son of a bitch hung."

"Very well, this jury is dismissed," Judge Coit said.

"Your Honor, you are declaring a mistrial?" Dexter asked.

Coit looked first at Davenport, then at Foster. "Declaring a mistrial would mean empaneling a new jury. And, like as not, we'd have the same problem with them as we had with this jury. No mistrial."

"No mistrial? Your Honor, you mean you are going to let the verdict, as brought by the jury, stand?" Foster asked.

Sue smiled broadly and spontaneously hugged Win. "We won!" she said.

"No, I don't think so," Dexter said in a quiet voice. He held his hand out. "Wait."

"I have decided to dismiss the jury and render a summary judgment," Coit said. "My summary judgment is guilty."

"What? Your Honor, you can't do that!" Dexter shouted. "I'm going to appeal!"

"You can appeal all you want, Mr. Davenport, but it will be too late to do your client any good. Mr. Coulter, I find you guilty, and I sentence you to hang by the neck until dead. That sentence to be carried out at four o'clock this afternoon. That is . . ." Coit looked up at the wall clock. "Two and one half-hours from now. May God have mercy on your soul."

Chapter 17

"STOP THAT!" THE LITTLE GIRL IN PIGTAILS CRIED.

The young boy who had tied the girl's pigtails together, ran away, giggling in delight.

"Mama, look what Johnny did," the little girl tattled.

"Johnny, if you don't behave yourself, I'm going to make you go home, and you won't get to see the hanging," Johnny's mother scolded.

"No, Mama, don't make me go home. I want to stay and watch," Johnny protested.

"Then stop pestering your little sister," the woman ordered.

"All right, I'll leave the little baby alone," Johnny said sarcastically, sticking his tongue out at his little sister, who stuck her tongue back at him. Leaving her and his mother, Johnny hurried over to join another group of young boys, all of whom were occupying a position in the very front of the crowd.

"You think he'll make a noise when he gets hung?" one of the boys asked.

"Nah, he can't make no noise," one of the others answered. "The rope'll be chokin' 'im, so he can't say a word."

"How much longer?"

"Don't know. Not much."

The gallows the boys were standing by was an unpainted, fresh-smelling structure built of new wood. A
stairway of thirteen steps led to the gallows floor. It
stood high and occupied a prominent position in the
middle of the street, right in front of the community
center, where earlier Win Coulter had been tried, convicted, and sentenced to hang.

It was not quite three-thirty, but already the crowd
was thick and jostling for position. There were men in
suits, shirtsleeves, and overalls, women in long dresses
and bonnets, and children, not only Johnny, his sister,
and the group of fascinated boys, but other, younger
children who threaded in and out of the crowd as they
chased one another around the gallows. A few enter-
prising vendors were selling lemonade, beer, pretzels,
popcorn, and sweet rolls.

Half a block away from the gallows, in the Horseshoe
jail, Elam, who by now had been given the position of
sheriff, was standing at the front window looking out
onto the street. Behind him, on the bunk in his cell, Win
sat, calmly paring an apple. One long, connected peel
hung down from the apple.

"Hey, look at this," he said enthusiastically. "This
may be the longest single peel I've ever done."

"What? Why are you doing that?" Sue asked in an
exasperated voice. "I can't believe this. They are about
to hang you and you . . . you are talking about a long
apple peel."

Both Sue and Dexter were in the cell with Win, allowed this privilege by Judge Coit because they were
his lawyers. Sue was standing by the window that looked
out over the alley behind the jail. Dexter was sitting on
an overturned water bucket.

"Well, long apple peels can sometimes pay off," Win

said easily. "I won a dollar once for having the longest peel. I beat Frank James by almost a full inch."

"Stop it!" Sue said, turning toward him. "Don't you understand what is about to happen to you?"

Win finished the peel, then lay it on the bunk beside him. He looked up at Sue.

"Of course I know what is about to happen to me, Sue," he said. "I'm about to be hanged."

"And you aren't concerned?"

"Not particularly."

"I don't understand that. You must be insane." Practically wringing her hands, Sue turned to her father. "Pa, we used the wrong tactic. We should have pled him not guilty by reason of insanity."

"I'm not insane, Sue," Win said, his voice still calm. "But you have to realize that I have faced the prospect of instant death for nearly all of my adult life. First in the war, and then in the life I have lived since the war. You can't be worrying about it all the time. So, I have made a conscious decision to treat death for what it is, a fact of life that is always there, waiting for all of us."

"That's an abstract concept," Sue said. "What I am talking about is real. It is right here, right now."

Win looked over at the clock on the wall of the sheriff's office. "No," he said, shaking his head. "It isn't here yet. I've got nearly half an hour remaining."

"Half an hour? Half an hour? Half an hour is nothing!"

"That's where you are wrong. The next half an hour is the rest of my life."

"No, I just can't accept that!" Sue wailed.

"Let's not give up hope yet, honey," Dexter said, speaking for the first time. "I've sent a telegram to Governor Bradley. In it, I made it clear, in no uncertain terms, that this trial was a total miscarriage of justice. And, you might be interested to know that Brigham Foster joined in the appeal."

"Foster did?" Win asked.

Dexter shook his head. "Foster is a good man. He prosecuted as vigorously as he could, because that was his job. But in the final analysis, he is a man of principle and ethical courage. He, too, believes the case should have been declared a mistrial."

"Why haven't we heard from the governor?" Sue asked. "We should have heard from him by now. Are you sure he hasn't answered?"

"Honey, as soon as he answers, we will know. Billy, down at Western Union, will run it down here immediately."

"Suppose Governor Bradley does grant us a stay, can we count on Judge Coit to abide by it?" Sue asked.

"He'll have to. If the governor orders a stay, Coit will have no choice but to comply," Dexter said. "Especially as Brigham Foster backs me on this."

The front door opened then and the hangman came in. He was smiling broadly.

"I'll bet there are three hundred people out there, waiting for the show," Tatum said to Elam and the others as he walked over to the coffeepot to pour himself a cup.

"That's what you call it? A show?" Sue asked.

"I call it a show, because that's what it is," Tatum said, coming over to stand just outside the cell. "Whenever somebody sees a hangin', why, that's somethin' that will stay with them for the rest of their lives. It's entertaining and educational. And it stars just two people. The hangman." He made a slight bow. "That's me. And the person gettin' hung." He swept one arm toward Win. "That's him."

"You actually enjoy this, don't you?" Sue asked incredulously.

"Oh, indeed I do, madam, indeed I do," Tatum said. "There's no greater satisfaction in life than for someone to take pleasure in the work they do. I take pleasure in my work, and I'm very good at it."

"What's good about it?" Dexter asked.

"The dignity of the moment," Tatum said. He looked again at Win, who, as yet, had not joined the conversation. "When I send you off to see your maker, Mr. Coulter, you can be sure that I'll do it in a dignified manner."

"Yeah, thanks," Win answered. "I'd been worried about that," he added sarcastically.

"Hey, Tatum," Elam called back from the front of the jail. "Here comes Judge Coit."

"Wonder what he wants?" Tatum asked.

"Pa! Maybe the stay has come through from the governor," Sue suggested excitedly.

"I don't know. It could be possible," Dexter said, showing some hope.

Win, who had now cut his apple into sections, began to eat it. He made no comment as to the possibility that the governor may have responded to Dexter's telegram, nor did he show any reaction.

When Coit came in, he walked straight over to the jail cell where he stood, alongside Tatum, just outside the cell. "Davenport, did you and Foster wire the governor behind my back?" he asked.

"Yes, we did," Dexter said. "Has there been an answer?"

Coit chuckled. "Oh yes, there's been an answer. It seems that the governor is an overnight guest for dinner at a nearby ranch, and they won't be able to deliver the message to him until he returns tomorrow. Looks like it's going to reach him too late to make any difference."

"Too late? What do you mean, too late?"

"Coulter's going to hang today," Coit said.

"Judge, surely you aren't going to go through with it now? You have the authority to delay this until tomorrow," Dexter said. "I beg of you to do so. Give us a chance to hear from the governor."

"I have no intention of changing my ruling. The execution takes place at four o'clock, as planned," Judge Coit said. He pulled a watch from his pocket and examined it. "That's less than fifteen minutes now. Sheriff Elam?"

"Yes, sir?"

"I suggest you get this prisoner down to the gallows. Mr. Tatum, it is time for you to go to work."

"It will be my honor," Tatum said.

Elam came over to the jail cell and opened the door. "All right, Dexter, Miss Davenport, you folks, come on out of there now," he said. "Your visitin' time is over."

With a dolorous expression on his face, Dexter looked at Win. Hesitantly, he stuck out his hand. "Good-bye, Mr. Coulter. I'm sorry I couldn't have done more for you."

Win shook it. "You've done all you could, and I've been grateful," he said.

Sue approached Win, started to hug him, then, unable to face him, turned away with a little sob. Dexter was providing what comfort he could for his daughter as they left the jail.

"Turn around," Elam ordered, and as Win did so, Elam tied his hands behind his back. "All right," he said. "Let's go."

With a shotgun poking into his back, Win walked the half block that separated the jail from the gallows. As he passed through the crowd of onlookers, he studied their faces. He saw pity in some, and horror in others, but morbid fascination in most. He smiled at a little girl with pigtails. Frightened, the little girl turned her face into her mother's skirt.

"Get up there," Elam growled, prodding him with sharp pokes in the back from the shotgun.

"Do you want a hood?" Tatum asked, holding up a piece of black cloth.

"No," Win replied. "When I get to hell, I want to look the devil right square in the face."

"Oohh," a woman in the front gasped at hearing such blasphemy.

In the distance a hawk called, and Win looked toward him and saw him flying free. Then an amazing thing happened. Win felt that somehow he and that bird had exchanged places, so that he was the one flying around, looking down on the proceedings. He felt totally detached from what was going on.

He reconnected with himself, though, when he saw Joe riding one horse toward the gallows and leading another. Joe was smoking a cigar and holding something in his hand. Win saw his brother touch the smoldering cigar to one of the objects in his hand, then throw it. That was when he realized that Joe was carrying several sticks of blasting powder.

As Joe was coming up behind the crowd, no one but Win had even noticed him. Therefore, when the first stick exploded, no one was expecting it, and there were several screams of surprise and fright. Almost immediately on the heels of the first explosion, there was a second, then a third.

"What is it? What's going on?" someone shouted.

Casually, and with a big grin spread across his face, Joe tossed a stick right in front of the gallows. It's sputtering fuse cleared out what was left of the crowd. He tossed still another stick up onto the gallows floor. It rolled across the floor to Win's feet, then stopped. Win could hear the fuse sparking and smell the burning cordite. Elam and the hangman were both on the gallows floor with Win.

"Holy shit!" Elam shouted, jumping off the edge of the gallows. Tatum, with his own cry of alarm, was right behind him.

"Get on," Joe said easily, leading the second horse right up to the gallows.

Win's hands were still tied behind him, but the height

of the gallows made it easy for him to just walk over and slip down onto the saddle.

"Hurry," Win said. "The fuse is almost down."

"Don't worry it," Joe replied with a chuckle. "That one isn't real." Joe rode away from the gallows then, still leading the second horse because Win, with his hands tied behind him, couldn't hold the reins.

They were no more than a few feet away when the stick of blasting powder Joe had tossed onto the gallows exploded. It went up with a roar, scattering shattered pieces of the lumber all over the center of town.

"Damn!" Win shouted, as chunks of wood, some of it rather large, rained down on them. "I thought you said that one wasn't real!"

"I must've gotten them mixed up," Joe said easily.

"That's a hell of a thing to get mixed up."

"You want to stay around here and talk about it, big brother? Or do you want to get the hell out of here?"

"Let's get the hell out of here," Win agreed, and using his legs for leverage, he held on as well as he could while Joe led them both out of town at a full gallop.

Chapter 18

"DO YOU SEE ANYTHING FROM THERE?" JOE CALLED. Win, who was clinging to the top of the telegraph pole looked back in the direction from which they had come.

"I'm not exactly riding the back of a hawk up here, Joe. I don't have that much better of a view than you do."

"Yeah, well I don't see anything from down here," Joe said. "I figured sure, they would be after us by now."

"Not if Elam has to get the posse together," Win replied. "He couldn't pour piss out of a boot if he had the instructions written on the heel." Win leaned around the pole and, using his knife, cut the telegraph wire. It fell to the ground with a twang, then Win climbed back down.

"There," he said. "This is the third section of wire we've removed. It'll take them a day or two to repair it. By the time they can send out any telegraph messages about us, we'll be well out of here. What do you say we head south, toward Arizona?"

Joe took a drink from his canteen, then screwed the top back on and hooked it across his saddle pommel.

"All right," Joe agreed. "But not until we go through Tybo."

"Tybo? Why do you want to go there?"

"For the same reason I wanted you to meet me there, instead of me coming to Reveille," Joe said. He opened his shirt pocket and took out the little peanut-sized nugget. "For this," he said, handing the nugget to his brother.

Win looked at it. "Damn, Joe," he said. "This is gold."

"It damn sure is," Win said as a wide grin spread across his face. "I told you I was goin' prospectin' while you were going to be gallivanting around back in Missouri. Well, I did go, and this is what I found. This . . . and a whole lot more like this."

"How much more?" Win asked.

"Well, if what Mr. Dempsey says is true, we might be talking in the neighborhood of fifty to a hundred thousand dollars or more."

"That's a pretty good neighborhood to be in," Win said.

"Yeah," Joe said. "That's what I was thinking."

"It won't do us much good, though, if we're picked up soon as we ride into Tybo," Win said.

"You've never been to Tybo, so the chances are you won't even be recognized," Joe said. "Besides, there's no posse comin' after us, and, like you said, we've cut the wire in a couple of places. It'll be a couple of days before word can even get out, and that's all we'll need."

"Then, lead on, McDuff, lead on," Win said as he swung into his saddle.

"McDuff," Joe said. "Yeah, I remember him. He was that redheaded guy from Springfield, wasn't he?"

Win laughed. "Yeah, something like that."

The two brothers spent the night on the trail and rode into Tybo early the next morning. As they passed by the cluster of small houses that sat just on the outskirts of town, a couple of women were talking back and forth as they hung out their wash. When they heard the hollow clump of hoofbeats, they halted their conversation and looked curiously over at Win and Joe. Smiling, Win touched the brim of his hat and nodded.

From those two houses, and the dozen or so others nearby, came the aroma of breakfast: bacon, coffee, eggs, and freshly baked biscuits.

Joe felt his stomach rumble with hunger.

By the time they reached the downtown area, a few of the merchants were already beginning their day's commerce. The hardware dealer raised dust with a vigorous use of his broom as he swept his front porch, while the grocer was using a chalkboard to post distress prices on the produce he had to move that day, or lose by spoilage. Both merchants nodded at the two brothers as they rode by.

A derelict, just awakening from his overnight drunk, pissed on the side of the leather goods store, totally unconcerned about his public exposure.

A dog scratched his fleas.

A prospector riding one mule and leading another, plodded down the street.

"Nobody has gotten excited over seeing us yet," Win suggested as they stopped in front of the Tybo Corral. The liveryman, still holding a cup of coffee came out to greet them. Wearing bib overalls and no shirt, he reeked, not only with body odor, but a few other, unidentifiable foul smells.

"How long?" he asked, as he took the reins.

"We'll do it day at a time until we know," Joe replied. He paid the fifty cents it required to board and feed both horses for one day and night.

"Rub them down," Win said.

"Always do," the stableman said. "It's part of the job."

When they stepped back outside, Joe pointed to a

building just up the street. "That's Little Man Lambert's Café," he said. "Why don't we have breakfast? If anybody is going to know anything about us, that's where we're going to find out."

Win chuckled. "Joe, if I didn't know you better, I'd say that was a good idea. But I know damn well that all you are thinking about right now is your stomach."

"Well, I am hungry," Joe said. "And you are, too, if you'd just admit it. Wait until you eat here. Little Man puts out the best breakfast I ever tasted."

"*Every* breakfast is the best breakfast you ever tasted," Win teased. As they approached the café, the aromas awakened Win's appetite as well, but he wasn't about to let Joe know that.

When Little Man saw Joe come into his café, he smiled broadly and hurried over to meet him.

"Hello, my friend!" Little Man said, shaking Joe's hand. "It's good to see you again."

"Hello, Little Man," Joe said. "I was telling my . . . uh, friend . . . here what a good breakfast you put out." Joe introduced Win as his friend, rather than brother, just in case word was out to look for two brothers.

"Coming from one with your appetite, I appreciate the compliment," Little Man said. "But if your friend eats like you do, I'm afraid I'll have to put on an extra shift in the kitchen."

Some of the nearby diners, particularly those who had been present the last time Joe had breakfast there, and who remembered Joe's prodigious appetite, laughed, and told the others what Little Man was talking about.

"You don't have to explain it to me, I've seen him eat before," Win said. "And believe me, I don't eat like he does. In fact, I'm not sure anyone eats like he does."

"Have a seat, gentlemen," Little Man said. "I'll bring you some coffee, then get the cook started on your breakfast. In fact, I'll probably have to help him."

Win and Joe took a table in the back of the room,

sitting with their backs to the wall, and in such a way as to afford them a view of the entire café and all its entrances.

"All right, Little Brother, this is your deal. So, what's your plan?" Win asked quietly as they took their seats.

"I thought we would go down to the assayer's office as soon as it opens," Joe replied. "By now he'll have the final report on what I brought in, and we'll be able to convert what I left with him to cash, over at the bank. That's one thousand dollars, less the hundred I got from Dempsey. Then, we'll go up to my claim and see what's there."

Win chuckled. "I've done a lot of things in my life, but I never thought I would be digging around like a miner."

"Miner?" Joe shook his head. "No, Win, that's the beauty of it. I didn't have to dig this stuff out. It was lying around loose, scattered in the dry chute of a creek bed. I just picked it up."

Little Man came over to their table then, carrying two cups and a coffeepot.

"Little Man, what time does the assayer's office open this morning?" Joe asked.

Little Man looked up at Joe with an expression of surprise on his face.

"The assayer's office?"

"Yes, Mr. Dempsey. What time does he open?"

"Oh, my friend, you mean you haven't heard?"

"Heard? Heard what?"

"It's a terrible thing. Ronald Dempsey was killed a couple of days ago."

"How?"

"He was murdered," Little Man said.

"Any idea who did it? Or why he was murdered?" Joe asked.

Little Man shook his head. "Nobody knows who it was, but ever'one thinks it was robbery. They say he had nearly a thousand dollars worth of gold in his office."

"Now, how would anyone know that?" Joe asked.

Little Man shrugged. "I don't know. I just know what ever'one is sayin'."

"What about his records?" Joe asked. "I filed on a claim a few days ago."

"Oh, you won't have any problem with that," Little Man said. "All of his records have been transferred to the land office. All you have to do is go down there with your claim number."

"That's good to know," Joe said.

"Have you got your claim number?" Win asked after Little Man left the table.

"Yep. I've got it right here," Joe said, patting the same shirt pocket where he was keeping his gold nugget. "We'll go down there after breakfast."

A moment later, Little Man began bringing out the first round of the boys' breakfast. Joe didn't disappoint Little Man, nor any of Little Man's patrons. His breakfast was of legendary proportions, and, as he was putting it away, Win overheard someone at one of the other tables.

"I told you so. Now pay up."

"I would never have believed you, if I hadn't seen it with my own eyes," an awed voice responded as he pulled out a silver dollar to pay off his wager.

After breakfast, Win and Joe started toward the land office to check on Joe's claim. They just stepped out of the café when they heard an excited shout.

"Coach is comin' in! Coach is comin' in!" a male voice called.

At the far end of the street, a coach, pulled by a team of six horses, came sliding around the corner then up the street. There was no real need to hold the team at a gallop, and indeed, when the coach was out on the road, the horses maintained a comfortable trot. But, as the

coming and going of the stagecoach was generally an
event of some interest to small, isolated towns such as
Tybo, the drivers invariably arrived and departed at a
gallop.

Followed by half-a-dozen running kids, the horses
pulled the coach at a very rapid clip up the street, hooves
pounding and wheels whirling, and throwing back a
rooster tail from the hard-packed dirt of Tybo's Main
Street.

"Whoa! Whoa!" the driver called to his team as the
coach approached the coach depot, which was just next
door to Little Man's. The driver hauled back on the reins
and pushed the brake lever forward with his right foot.
The wheels began to skid, and the horses came to a
shuddering stop, then stood there, blowing hard, shaking
their manes and stomping their feet, trying to bleed off
the energy that had sustained them for the last several
miles.

"Tybo, folks!" the driver called. He tied off his reins,
then climbed down. "This here is Tybo!"

The driver opened the coach door and four passengers
stepped out of the stage. None of the passengers meant
anything to Joe, but Win saw them and he drew a gasp
of surprise.

"I'll be damned," he said.

"What is it?"

Win pointed to two of the passengers. "That's Dexter
and Sue Davenport," he said.

Neither Dexter nor Sue had eaten their breakfast, so,
after introductions, the four of them returned to Little
Man's. Joe ordered a stack of pancakes for himself.

"Joe, don't tell me you are still hungry," Win said.

"Well, I'm not really. But I don't like to see anyone
have to eat alone. Are you going to eat that bacon?" he
asked, when he saw Sue push it aside.

"No," Sue answered. "Do you want it?"

"Not really, but I reckon it would be a shame for it

to go to waste," Joe said, reaching for it. He ate it in three bites.

"I'm really surprised to see you here. Pleased, but surprised," Win said. "How did you know where to find me?"

"The first day we met, you said you were on your way to Tybo to meet your brother when someone shot your horse," Dexter said.

"That's right, I was. Yeah, I guess I do remember telling you that," Win said. He took a swallow of his coffee and studied Dexter over the rim of his coffee. "I guess I just didn't think you would remember it."

"It's easy to see why you would think that I wouldn't remember," Dexter said. "As I recall, I was pretty hung-over that day. But then, I've been hungover every day now for nearly two years. Except for today."

"So, you knew where to look for me. The next question is, why have you come after me? I hope you don't have some notion of trying to talk me into going back."

Sue laughed, and Dexter shook his head. "Heavens no," he said. "I'd never do that to you. Especially since I have this," Dexter said, taking a paper from his jacket pocket.

"What is that?" Win asked.

"It's a telegram from Governor Bradley, granting you a stay of execution, pending a new trial."

Win laughed. "That's nice, but if Joe hadn't taken a hand, the governor's stay would have arrived too late. I am curious, though. How did you get the message? We cut the wires as we left Horseshoe."

Dexter chuckled. "Believe me, I know . . . I tried to send a telegram ahead to Tybo, to tell you about the stay. The truth is, Win, this wire arrived *before* you left. Judge Coit knew about it all along, but he decided to ignore it. Instead, he came up with that cock and bull story about the governor being out of reach."

"Why would he do that?" Win asked.

Dexter shook his head. "He obviously wanted you dead. Have you ever crossed paths with Judge Coit?"

"Not that I know of."

"Well, for some reason, he seems to have it in for you."

"I don't know what you did when you got back from Missouri, Big Brother, but you sure got a heap of folks mad at both of us. First, those fellas back in Reveille tried to kill you, then there were those two sidewinders who came at me with knives . . . then somebody killed your horse and left you to die, and your run-in with Taggert, and the little fracas I had with Anders and Jacoby."

"Wait a minute," Sue said. "Joe, did you say you had a run-in with Anders and Jacoby?"

"Yes. Why, do you know them?" Joe asked.

"Oh yes, I know them," Sue answered. She shivered. "I know one of them too well," she added.

"They are also court deputies," Dexter added. "They both work for Judge Coit."

"Actually, only one of them works for Coit," Joe said.

"No, both of them do," Sue insisted.

Joe shook his head. "Now, only Jacoby does. I killed Ben Anders," he said, matter-of-factly. "You going to eat that biscuit?"

Chapter 19

IT HAD BEEN LESS THAN AN HOUR AFTER JOE'S BOLD rescue of his brother when Dexter Davenport learned about the stay of execution. At first, Dexter, angry by what happened, was going to confront Coit with the information. But Sue had a cooler head, reminding him that if Coit knew about it and didn't stop the hanging, then he might be dangerous to them as well.

Dexter agreed, and without disclosing their intentions to anyone, he and Sue took the next coach out of Horseshoe. They weren't sure Win and Joe would be in Tybo, but they did know that was where Win was headed when his horse was shot. And that information, they kept to themselves.

At ten o'clock the previous night, after a long, grinding ride over rough roads, the coach stopped at a way-station. There, they were given a meal of bacon, beans, and corn bread. Afterward, Dexter, Sue, and the other passengers slept fitfully on wooden benches in the waiting room. The hostler provided blankets for free, but the pillows rented for ten cents.

Two hours before dawn that morning, the coach got under way again, arriving in Tybo a little after eight. As a result of their long, hard trip, both Dexter and Sue were very tired so, after breakfast, they took rooms in the hotel.

As the four of them checked in, Win paid particular attention to the room assignments. Sue was in room 211.

"We'll see you later today, after we've had a little rest," Dexter said as he and his daughter started toward the stairs. "In the meantime, you boys stay out of trouble."

"Well, if we do get into trouble, I know a couple of pretty good lawyers," Win said.

Dexter looked genuinely pleased by Win's response. "Thanks," he said.

"No, Mr. Davenport. I thank you."

Leaving the hotel, the two brothers walked along the sidewalk to the Land Office, their boots clumping loudly on the wide-plank boards. As they passed the notions shop, a woman stepped out in front of them. Joe recognized her immediately.

"Hello, Lucy," Joe said, touching the brim of his hat.

"Joe, you've come back!" Lucy said, squealing in delight.

"I couldn't stay away," Joe teased.

"You broke my heart, you know," Lucy said, extending her lower lip in a faux pout.

"Did I?"

"You did indeed."

Win laughed. "You'll have to excuse Joe, miss. That's just the way he is. Why, if you just knew how he was, you wouldn't have anything to do with him. He has left a string of broken hearts all over the West."

"I'm sure he has," Lucy replied. Then, noticing Win, she smiled seductively. "And you have too, I'd be willing to bet," she added flirtatiously. "Where are your manners, Joe? Aren't you going to introduce me to this very handsome gentleman?"

"This is my brother, Win."

"Your brother? Oh, my, I can certainly see that attractive men run in the family. I do hope the two of you are going to come see me while you are here."

"I'll come see you, all right," Joe said. He nodded toward Win. "But as far as I'm concerned, Win can get his own girl."

"I don't think he'll have any trouble doing just that." Lucy turned her attention back to Joe. "I'm counting on you coming to see me, just real soon." She looked at Win. "With, or without your brother."

With a toss of her curls, Lucy hurried on down the boardwalk.

"I see you made a friend while you were here," Win said as they continued their walk.

"Well, you know me, Win. I'm a real friendly person."

"Uh huh," Win replied laconically. He pointed to a building just in front of them. "There it is. Nye County Land Office."

The land office was a small, two-room lean-to shack that protruded from the side of the bank. Just inside the door was a counter that ran three-quarters of the way across the room. The north and east walls had windows, through which spilled a bright splash of sunlight. The west wall, which was actually the east wall of the bank building itself, was plastered with maps of Nye County. The back wall was lined with shelves. A door on the back wall led into another room.

Win stepped over to study the maps. Nye County was so large that it required four map sections to cover it.

"Where is this claim of yours?" Win asked.

"Right here," Joe said, pointing to one of the maps. "In the Monitor Mountains."

"Hard to get there?"

"It's not a leisurely ride, but if we leave early in the morning, we should get there before nightfall," Joe said.

Win looked around the still empty room. "Wonder

where everyone is? It doesn't look as if anyone is that interested in doing business with us," he suggested.

"Maybe they didn't hear us. Hello? Anyone here?" Joe called.

There was a scurrying sound from the back room, then someone came through the door. "Sorry, gentlemen, I was busy and didn't hear you come in," the land clerk apologized. He saw that they were looking at the maps. "Studying Nye County, are you? If you are looking to homestead, we have some choice sections available down in Oasis Valley. That's right about here," he said, crossing over to the map and pointing to the southern part of the county.

"We aren't looking to homestead," Joe said.

"Oh?" the clerk replied. "Then you are buying property somewhere? Excellent idea, sir. Some of the earlier property has been improved quite nicely."

"Not looking to buy, either," Joe said. "I've come to pick up the papers to my mining claim."

"Mining claim? Oh, yes," the clerk said. "I'm sorry, I guess I still haven't gotten used to the fact that those records are being kept here now. They were moved down right after poor Mr. Dempsey was shot." He took a large notebook down from a shelf, blew the dust from it, then opened it. Removing his glasses, he began to polish them with his handkerchief. He looked up at Joe. "Do you have your claim number?"

"Yes," Joe said. "The claim number is two-five-one-four."

The clerk put his glasses back on. "Two-five-one-four," he repeated as he opened the notebook. Licking his fingers he turned several pages until he got to the page he was looking for. He ran his finger down the long column of numbers. "Ah, here it is. Two-five-one-four. Located up in the Monitor Range, I believe?"

"That's it," Joe said. He smiled excitedly at Win.

The clerk moved his finger over to the right side of

the page. "According to this, the claim papers haven't returned from the county seat at Belmont."

Joe's face reflected his frustration and disappointment. "Not back yet? Why not? How long does it take to post the claim?"

"I know that property deeds normally return within a week," the clerk said. "But I really don't have any experience in dealing with mineral claims. If you are concerned, though, you could send a telegram to the claims office in Belmont and make an inquiry."

"Yes," Joe said. "Yes, we might just do that. Thank you."

"Not at all," the land clerk replied. "Oh, and if your mine doesn't work out and you decide to go into farming, come back and see me. There are still some choice pieces of land remaining for anyone who will apply himself."

"Yeah, thanks again," Joe said.

Leaving the land office, Win and Joe went directly to the Western Union office.

"Good morning, Mr. Stone," Joe said.

"Good morning," Stone replied. He stared at Joe. "I know you, don't I? Didn't I send a telegram for you a few days ago?"

"No," Joe said. "You sold me a nostrum for a toothache."

Stone laughed. "A nostrum for a toothache," he said. "Very good. Yes, very good indeed."

Win looked at Joe with a quizzical expression on his face.

"It's an inside joke," Joe explained, reaching for one of the message pads. He carefully wrote his message and then handed it to Stone.

"How long you think it'll be before I hear back from them?" he asked.

"From the clerk of claims and deeds?" Stone replied. He looked up at the clock on the wall. "Knowing how they work, it'll take 'em a while before they get around to even reading your message. Then they'll have to go through the records. I doubt you'll hear anything back from them before mid to late afternoon."

"Then we'll see you this afternoon," Joe said.

"You take care of that toothache now," Stone called out, laughing at the joke.

Once outside, Joe rubbed his hands together and smiled. "Well, nothing to do now but wait," he said. "So what do you say we pay a call on Lucy and some of her friends?"

"And just what kind of call would that be, Little Brother? Social or business?" Win asked.

"Win, with ladies like Lucy and her friends, social calls *are* business calls."

Win chuckled. "That's what I thought."

"I like it like that. There's no misunderstanding, no beating around the bush. You know what you want, and they know what you want. So, what do you say? Shall we make that visit?"

"You go ahead," Win said. "I think I'll just wander around on my own for a while."

"Have it your own way," Joe said easily. "But as for me, when I've got a couple of hours to kill and a room waiting, it's nice to have a willing woman to keep you company."

Win didn't disagree with his brother. The only place they parted company was on the choice of a willing woman. Win had his own choice in mind. What he didn't know was whether or not his choice would be willing.

Returning to the hotel, Win climbed the stairs up to the long, carpeted hallway of the second floor. Although three kerosene lanterns burned in the hallway, their chimneys were so blackened with smoke that the light was very dim, thus causing the hallway to be quite dark.

The doors to each room had been red at one time, though the paint was so distressed and flecked that it was hard to tell the color. The door numbers, in faded white, were difficult, but not impossible to read.

Win stopped just outside 211 and knocked lightly.

"Just a minute," a voice answered.

The door was pushed open just a crack, and Win saw Sue peering through. When she saw that it was Win, she exhibited a brief moment of surprise, which gave way to a broad smile. Stepping away from the door, she opened it to let him in. As soon as Win was inside, Sue stuck her head out into the hall and looked both ways. Satisfied that no one had seen him enter, she closed the door.

"I was hoping you would come," she said. Sue was wearing a white-cotton nightgown, which, though opaque, was so thin that he could see the impressions her nipples made in the soft cloth as it draped across her breasts.

"I wasn't sure you would be interested in, uh, company," Win said.

"Oh, I'm interested," Sue said. "The fact is, you got my comb red the first time I ever saw you." Without another word, she crossed her arms, grabbed a handful of cloth, then pulled her nightgown over her head. As a result of that action, she was standing before him, completely, beautifully, and unashamedly, naked. "The question is, are you interested?" she asked.

Win let out a long, slow, whistling breath. "Yes, indeed. I would say that I am very interested."

"Win, I know you must consider me a brazen hussy," Sue said. "First, by the way I kissed you when I first met you in jail, and now this. But I can't help myself."

"No, I don't consider you a hussy at all. Just friendly," Win replied, smiling at her. He put his hands on her breasts, then bent over to brush his lips across them, moving from one to the other.

Sue's body began twitching in pleasure, and she put her hands behind Win's head, pulling him to her, guiding him from side to side. Then, even as he was kissing her breasts and sucking her nipples, Win began undoing his trousers and pushing them and his underwear down to the floor.

Sue helped him get undressed, then she grabbed his swelling shaft and squeezed it.

"Oh my," she breathed. "I guess you really are interested, aren't you?"

"I told you I was," Win said. "And I never lie to a beautiful naked lady."

Sue laughed. "Why is it that I believe you have seen a lot of beautiful naked ladies?"

"Doesn't matter how many I've seen," Win said. "I'm only looking at one now." He picked her up and carried her over to the bed. Lying beside her, he put his hand on her inner thigh, then moved it up. He slid his finger through the lips of her sex, feeling the slickness of her desire. She moaned with pleasure and, grabbing his penis, began moving her hand up and down his shaft, feeling its throbbing heat. For fully a minute, Win's fingers teased, probed, stroked, and massaged until Sue was squirming in uncontrollable desire.

"Win," she finally said, her voice trembling with passion. "Win, please . . . I can't stand the agony. I want you in me now."

Obliging her, Win moved his body over hers. As he lowered himself into position, Sue guided him into the accommodating damp folds of flesh that hid the center of her womanhood. It was well lubricated with the copious flowing of her sex and when Sue put her hands behind Win's butt and pulled forward, he slipped in easily. She thrust up against him and pulled him deeper into her.

"Oh, yes!" she said in one long sigh of ecstasy.

Win felt as if he had just dipped his wick in a vat of

hot wax. It was a wonderful, delicious sensation, and as Sue writhed in her own rapture beneath him, he put his mouth to her neck. He could feel her neck muscles twitching, and he opened his mouth to suck on the creamy white flesh. He could hear the gasps and moans of pleasure from this beautiful creature beneath him, and she continued to raise her hips wildly to meet his every thrust.

Win heard Sue's gasps and moans rise in intensity, and he could tell by the increase in her movements and the spasmodic action of her hips that she was nearing orgasm. He rode with her, and when she peaked, her contractions sucked the juices from deep within Win's body. It was a total, all-consuming orgasm, and for an instant he felt keenly with every inch of his body that was in contact with Sue's naked skin.

Win lay on top of Sue for a few seconds, then rolled to one side. He put his arm out and Sue cuddled against it. His hand was positioned just over her breast, and Sue reached up and brought it down so he could massage it.

"All the time we were in court, I was imagining this," Sue said. "I knew it would be like this. I just knew it would."

Chapter 20

LUCY MET JOE IN THE DOWNSTAIRS DRAWING ROOM OF the sporting house where she worked, then led him upstairs to her room. From his position behind her, Joe could watch her butt wriggle inside the snug fit of the dress she was wearing.

"My room is down the hall . . ." Lucy said.

"On the left," Joe interrupted. "I remember."

"You do? I'm flattered," Lucy said. "I'm sure you've been in your share of such rooms."

Lucy unlocked the door, then pushed it open, inviting Joe to go in first. The room, just as Joe remembered, was considerably larger than a normal hotel room. It was dominated by a four-poster bed, covered with a bright comforter. There were curtains to match, hanging at the windows.

The windows on the back wall looked out onto a freight company, its yards busy with departing and arriving wagons.

"You just going to stand there all day?" Lucy asked. "Or is there something I could do that might get you interested in me?"

When Joe turned back around, he saw her working on

the buttons at the back of her gown. She watched him
with smoky eyes and a provocative grin as she undid
the last button and let the gown fall to her waist, exposing her large breasts. She started pushing the gown
down over her hips, squirming as she did so, causing
her breasts to jiggle.

"You plannin' on doin' this with all your clothes on?"
Lucy asked.

Joe grinned crookedly. "I guess it would be better if
I shucked out of them," he said.

Joe was out of his clothes so quickly that Lucy barely
had time to flip the scarlet coverlet back. Then they were
in bed together and, without any further preliminaries,
he moved on top of her as her legs went around his waist
and her hands slid up from his ribs to grab him just
below the shoulders. Then, reaching down, she helped
him make the connection. He pushed in, hot and hard,
deep into her, then pulled back slowly and held himself
for a second before thrusting into her again. After that,
he established a steady pace of long, powerful thrusts
and withdrawals.

Supporting himself above her with his hands, he enjoyed the perspective, watching every thrust as it rever-
berated through her, her big breasts jiggling, erect
nipples pointing up at him. He managed to keep himself
just below climax, pacing himself so it would last, so he
could bring her with him.

Joe felt Lucy's fingernails rake down across his ribs,
saw her grin widen to a pleased leer as he jerked in
response. He took her with him, right up to where he
was, hanging on the edge, hot and blood-pounding with
lust.

Joe slid one arm under the small of her back, lifting
her up from the bed until only her shoulders touched the
sheet. He began thrusting deeper into her, long and slow
and powerful, feeling that hot lust raging through his
brain, driving and driving into her until he saw her eyes

close, saw her hands come down to clutch at the sheet, saw her head begin to rock from side to side, her lower lip caught between her teeth.

And then the little cries began to come from her; he felt her ankles lock across his back, her hands clutch the bed for leverage, and her hips pumping frantically. For a moment he held her to a slower pace, never losing contact with her until, finally he let her go and felt her surge into wild rapid lunging.

Joe caught up to her pace, surpassed it, mastered it, then mastered her, his own eyes closing from the heat of it. Through the blood pounding in his own ears he heard her wild cries as she surged up in frantic rhythm that brought her up and over. He came after her, lunging and thrashing in a long final frenzy that brought them both back down on the bed. He felt her hands snake up around his neck, felt those big breasts heaving against his chest, felt her shudder up against him, shudder down again, and then leech herself to him in one final prolonged quiver, all her sleek round curves soft against his skin.

They lay that way for what seemed like a long time, on their sides, her head tucked down under his. He was still in the warm hollow of her thighs, her legs around his waist. A faint breeze stirred curtains at the open window, welcome because it was well into the heat of the day.

Lucy grinned and slid a sharp fingernail up his chest. "You know, a fella like you could make me forget I'm even in the business. This one is on the house."

Joe laughed, then shook his head. "Huh uh," he said. "When I get my money's worth of anything, I expect to pay for it." He reached for his pants. "And, darlin', you gave me my money's worth."

"Too bad you can't take advantage of a special offer I have," Lucy said.

"Now, what offer would that be?"

"My two-for-one sale."

Joe put the money on a bedside table, then smiled at her. "And just what makes you think I can't take advantage of it?" he asked, moving down to take one of her nipples into his mouth.

"Oh, my," Lucy said, feeling him growing again. "You *are* quite a man!"

One hour later, Win, Joe, Sue, and Dexter were having lunch together at Little Man's. Sue was bubbly and almost openly flirtatious with Win. A couple of times, Win caught Dexter looking at him, the expression in Dexter's eyes indicating that he suspected something may have happened between Win and Sue. That same expression, however, said that Dexter, who was just beginning to put his own life back together, wasn't about to criticize his daughter for anything she might have done.

After lunch, the four of them walked over to the telegraph office to see if there was any reply to Joe's telegram.

"I've got it right here," Arnold Stone said, handing Joe the message sheet. "I've got a feeling this isn't what you expected, though."

"What do you mean?" Joe asked, looking at Stone suspiciously.

"Maybe you'd better read it," Stone suggested.

Joe read it to himself. "What the hell?" he said.

"Read it aloud, Joe," Win said.

"This will confirm that all mineral rights, surface and subterranean, now relating to claim 2514 in the Monitor Mountain range henceforth and for a period of forty years, appertains to Judge Preston Coit," Joe read.

"What?" Win asked.

Joe looked up from the telegram. "How the hell did that son of a bitch get my claim?"

"I don't know," Dexter replied. "But the fact that he has explains a few things. Win, Judge Coit wasn't trying you. He was using the law to steal your brother's claim and to murder you."

"And he damn near did it," Win said.

"Yes, but what I want to know is . . . how the hell did he know I had filed a claim in the first place?" Joe asked.

"Yes, and how did he know about me? He not only knew I was your brother, he knew exactly where to find me."

"I might be able to answer that," Stone said.

Joe looked at the telegrapher. "What do you mean?"

Stone cleared his throat. "I, uh, am supposed to be sworn to secrecy," he said. "I'm not supposed to ever reveal anything that I send or receive. But, Mr. Jacoby does represent the law so I, uh, thought it would be all right."

"What are you talking about?" Dexter asked.

"Marshal Moe Jacoby asked me about you," Stone said to Joe. "He knew you had sent a telegram to someone, and he wanted to know who you sent it to."

"You told him, I suppose?"

"What was I to do?" Stone asked. "As I said, he is an officer of the court. I figured I didn't have any choice in the matter."

"Yes, but how did he even know to ask?" Joe asked. "I didn't say anything in the telegram about the claim."

"Maybe you didn't, but Dempsey did," Stone said. "He was all excited about it, and he sent a wire to the county clerk of claims and deeds, telling about the ore that was brought in."

"When did he do that?"

Stone started looking through his records. "Here it is," he said. "He sent his telegram on the same day you sent yours. There was less than an hour between them."

"You said Jacoby asked about Mr. Coulter," Dexter said. "By any chance, did Jacoby send a telegram?"

"Yes, I believe he did send one," Stone said. "It was in answer to a message he received from Judge Coit."

"He got one from Coit? What did that one say?" Win asked.

Stone shook his head. "I'm sorry, that was official county business. I can't tell you that."

"Mr. Stone, you know those toothache nostrums they sell next door?" Joe asked.

"Yes?" Stone replied, guardedly.

"If you don't help us out here, there won't be enough nostrums in the entire apothecary to take care of you."

Intimidated by Joe's inference, Stone, with shaking hands, began riffling through his filed messages until he came up with one. "This is the one that came from Judge Coit," he said.

GOLD FOUND NEAR TYBO. CLAIM FILED BY JOE COULTER.

Win read the message, then passed it around to the others.

"What did Jacoby say in answer?" Joe asked.

Stone handed yet another message over to Joe.

INFORMATION HERE IS THAT JOE COULTER HAS BROTHER IN REVEILLE NAMED WIN. WILL TAKE CARE OF THE SITUATION.

"I can't believe they would actually put in the telegram that they are going to try and kill us," Joe said.

Dexter chuckled and shook his head. "My boy, you should look at things with a lawyer's eyes," he suggested. "Whereas we don't have the slightest doubt as to what they are talking about, there is not one intimidating word in either of those telegrams."

Ten minutes later, the four were discussing all their options at a table in a saloon called The Tybo Watering Hole.

"Here you are. Three beers and one . . ." the waiter paused, then let the word slide out derisively. "Sarsparilla. You are a little old for this kind of drink, aren't you, mister?"

The four had just ordered drinks, and it was Dexter's request for a sarsparilla that brought on the waiter's sarcasm.

"Waiter," Joe said easily. "Is there a good doctor in this town?"

"Yes, there's ole Doc Kincaid. He has an office over the general store. Why?" He glanced toward Dexter. "Are you afraid the sarsparilla is too strong for your friend?" The waiter laughed at his own joke.

"No," Joe said. "I was just wondering who we could summon to pull my boot out of your ass."

The waiter looked at Joe as if about to respond, then noticing Joe's size, made a quick reassessment of his options. He chose the wiser course.

"I'll, uh . . . be over there if you need any more drinks," he said, beating a hasty retreat.

Dexter laughed. "Watching the expression on that man's face was almost worth having to drink this," he said, holding the soft drink in front of him and studying it without enthusiasm. "If I am honest with myself, I'll never again drink anything any stronger than this."

Sue put her hand on her father's arm. "I'm very proud of you, Pa," she said.

Dexter put his hand on his daughter's. "That, alone, is enough to make me drink this stuff." He took a swallow. "It's not all that bad," he said as he screwed his face up in distaste.

The others laughed.

"Joe, when you found the ore, did you make a quick claim?" Dexter asked.

"Yes, I did."

"Were there any witnesses?"

"No. I just wrote it out on a piece of paper, signed it, put it in a tin can, and buried it."

"Too bad there weren't any witnesses," Dexter said. "If there are witnesses to a quick claim, and that quick claim pre-dates a filing with the office of claims and deeds, the quick claim will be accepted as the more valid of the two documents."

"Why don't we witness it?" Sue asked.

Dexter shook his head. "We can't," he answered. "As I said, the date of witnessing must precede the date of filing."

"Who would know?" Sue asked.

"I would know," Dexter replied. "And as an officer of the court, for me to do such a thing would be the same thing as committing perjury."

"You would let something like that stand in your way, even though you know that Coit and Jacoby are stealing the claim from Joe?" Sue asked.

Dexter shook his head, then looked across the table at Win and Joe. "I'm sorry, Win, Joe," he said. "I hope you understand."

"Don't worry about it," Win said easily. "I'm pretty sure we'll find Coit and Jacoby out at Joe's claim. And if they are there, we'll just have a face-to-face meeting with them. I'm sure we will be able to negotiate a solution to our problems."

"Would you let me go with you?" Sue asked.

"Sue, don't talk nonsense," Dexter said. "Coit and Jacoby are dangerous men."

"Jacoby was one of the men who raped me," Sue said. "And I know now that Coit not only knew it, he countenanced it. He denied us justice the last time, but I will have my day in court."

"Then I'm going, too," Dexter said.

"Pa, there's no need for you to put yourself in danger."

"You don't really think I would let you go by yourself, do you?"

"I won't be by myself. Win and Joe will be with me. That is . . . if you will let me go," she added, looking directly at Win.

"I never try and talk another person out of doin' what has to be done," Win said. "If you want to come with us, come ahead. That goes for both of you," he added."

"Then, I'm coming as well," Dexter insisted.

Chapter 21

JOE LED WIN, SUE, AND DEXTER INTO THE MONITOR Mountain range, to the general area where he had made his gold find and staked his quick claim. It was dark by the time they got there and, ahead of them, they could see the faint glow of a campfire. Joe pointed out that the campfire was almost exactly where his claim was.

"You think its Coit and Jacoby?" Sue asked.

"Could be. Why don't you two wait here while Joe and I take a look," Win said. His suggestion, which was more in the form of an order, wasn't questioned.

Pistols in hand, Win and Joe started toward the glow of the campfire. Within seconds they were swallowed up by the darkness so that Sue and Dexter, even though they knew Win and Joe were nearby, suddenly felt as if they were all alone.

An owl hooted.

A distant coyote called.

The wind whistled.

Sue shivered.

"Are you cold or afraid?" Dexter asked.

"A little of both," Sue admitted.

"Yes," Dexter replied. He put his arm around his daughter. "Me too."

A quarter of a mile away, Win and Joe were moving quickly through the night. By now they were close enough to the glowing campfire to overhear voices and Win reached out to touch his brother in a signal to stop.

"That's Coit's voice," he whispered.

"I can't believe you could be so damn dumb that you didn't even check this out," they heard Coit saying in a loud, angry voice.

"You didn't say anything about checking out the claim site," another voice answered. "All you said was to take care of the Coulter brothers."

"Yes, well, you couldn't even do that, could you?" Coit said.

"The Coulters ain't ordinary men."

"I only heard Jacoby's voice one time," Joe whispered. "But that sounds like him."

"Are you saying there's no gold here at all?" a third voice asked. Neither Win nor Joe were able to recognize the voice.

"That's what I'm saying," Coit replied. "We've done all this for nothing."

"But what about the ore Coulter brought in?" Jacoby asked. "Before I killed Dempsey, he told me he was holdin' at least a thousand dollars' worth. Where did that come from?"

"Yeah, that had to come from somewhere," still a fourth voice said. "It didn't just drop out of the sky."

"As a matter fact, it did fall from the sky," Coit said.

"What do you mean if fell from the sky?" Jacoby asked.

"Five years ago the Culpepper mine had about a week's worth of ore, all dug up waiting to be hauled out. They also had a lot of powder on hand, to use to open up another shaft. Somehow the powder exploded and it caused a rock slide, including the ore. From time to time, some of that ore is still being found. Coulter just happened to stumble across a little pocket of it, that's all. He thought he had hit the mother lode. In fact, all he found was a scrap pile."

"Did he get all of it?" By now, Win and Joe were close enough to see the four men sitting around the campfire. "Maybe there's some left."

"Anders had more gold in that tooth of his than there is here," Coit replied.

"No gold? Damn," Joe said quietly. "And all this time I thought we were rich."

"Which one is Jacoby?" Win asked.

"He's the short, hairy son of a bitch," Joe said. "Oh, and I've run across those other two bastards, too. They are the ones who jumped me in Reveille."

Suddenly a fifth voice called out. The voice came from the dark, from the left, or south side of the campfire, Win and Joe having approached the fire from the east.

"Judge! Don't shoot! I'm comin' in, and I've got some people with me!"

"Who the hell is that?" Joe asked.

"Sounds like Elam's voice," Win replied.

"Come on in, Elam," Coit called back, confirming Win's suspicion.

Win and Joe watched as three figures moved into the golden bubble of light.

"Oh shit!" Win said.

Walking in front of Elam, with their hands raised, were Dexter and Sue Davenport.

"Only one of us should've come," Joe said. "The other one of us should have stayed with them."

"Too late to worry about that now," Win replied.

"Well, well, if it isn't two thirds of Horseshoe's legal community," Coit said in a sarcastic welcome. "Where did you find them?"

"I found them about a quarter of a mile back," Elam said.

"What are you doing up here?" Coit asked.

"As you know, I haven't had that much success as a lawyer lately," Dexter said. "So we came up here to prospect for gold."

Coit laughed, a sharp, brittle laugh. "I have to hand it to you, Mr. Davenport, you do have a droll sense of humor." The smile left his face. "I'll ask you again. What are you doing here?"

"There's two more out there somewhere," Elam said. "I found four horses."

"Four horses, you say? Interesting. Who is with you?" he asked. "Where are the others?"

"Nobody came with us," Dexter answered. "The other two horses are packhorses, in case we found gold."

"Packhorses with saddles?" Elam scoffed. "Who are you kidding?"

"I must give you credit, Mr. Davenport. You are displaying more courage than one might expect from a drunken fool."

"My father is no longer a drunk," Sue said resolutely.

"Perhaps not. But he is still a fool. All four of you are, thinking you could get the better of me. Now, who is with you?"

"Whoever it is, I'll get them in," Jacoby said. He drew his pistol and pointed it at Sue's head. Sue closed her eyes tightly.

"Jacoby! No!" Dexter shouted. "If you must shoot someone, shoot me!"

"Oh, I will," Jacoby replied. "I'm going to shoot both of you if your two friends don't come in with their hands up . . . right now."

"Judge Coit! You can't let this happen!" Dexter pleaded.

Coit shrugged his shoulders. "I'm like Pontius Pilate," he said. "I wash my hands of this. I'm sure you know that Mr. Jacoby is a man with a violent nature. If he says he is going to shoot your daughter unless your friends show themselves, then I have no doubt that he will."

"If anyone is out there," Jacoby said. "This is your last chance."

After Jacoby's call there was a beat of silence, broken by the sound of the cylinder being engaged as he pulled the hammer back.

"No, please!" Dexter shouted.

"Hold it!" Win called from outside the bubble of light. "Don't shoot her. We're coming in!"

With their hands raised, Win and Joe emerged from the darkness.

"It's good to see you again, Mr. Coulter," Coit said to Win. Jacoby was still holding the pistol to Sue's head. "Or, should I say the misters Coulter, since you are obviously Joe Coulter."

Joe said nothing.

"You may lower the pistol, Mr. Jacoby."

Jacoby lowered his gun.

"You are the son of a bitch that nearly blinded me," one of the men said bitterly, looking at Joe. His face, as well as the face of the man standing next to him, was discolored with bruises.

"I'm sure you recognize these two gentlemen," Coit said, nodding toward the two men. "When I learned you had gone to Reveille, I sent Mr. Pugh and Mr. Chandler here to kill you. They failed, and I must say, they came out somewhat the worse for their encounter with you."

"That's what happens when you send boys to do a man's job," Joe said.

"Critchlow, Tombs, Anders, Taggert . . . they're dead too, because of the two of you."

"Judge, what do you want to do with them?" Elam asked.

"I know what I aim to do with this one," Jacoby said. He looked at her with eyes that were deep and evil.

Reflecting the flickering light of the flames, it was like looking into hell itself. Shivering, Sue moved toward her father. Dexter put his arm around her.

"No need goin' to your daddy, little girl," Jacoby said. "He can't help you." Jacoby rubbed himself. "It was good last time . . . but it's goin' to be even better this time."

"Don't you touch her," Dexter said.

Jacoby laughed. "You couldn't do anything about it last time, what makes you think you can this time?"

"That's enough of that," Coit said. "Mr. Elam, you raised a good question. What are we going to do with them?" He looked toward Win. "Of course, Mr. Win Coulter's fate has already been decided. I sentenced him to hang, and he is going to do just that." He looked at Joe. "And so will this one, for interfering in the discharge of a court-ordered execution."

"You can't hang them," Dexter said. "The governor granted a stay, pending a new trial. And everyone in Horseshoe knows that by now."

"An astute observation, Mr. Davenport, but I have no intention of returning to Horseshoe," Coit said. "As a circuit judge, I have the authority to incorporate a community anywhere three or more people request incorporation. Gentlemen . . . and lady," he said, with a deferential nod toward Sue, "I hereby incorporate this site as the town of Goldslide. And, until such time as an election can be conducted, I appoint you, Mr. Pugh, as the mayor, and you, Mr. Chandler, as the town marshal. Gentlemen, disarm the prisoners and carry out the sentence."

Grinning, the newly appointed "marshal" and "mayor" started toward Win and Joe with guns drawn. Dexter, who had moved slowly, and unobserved, toward the fire, suddenly kicked up a burning brand. Glowing cinders went into Elam's eyes, and with a shout of pain, he dropped his pistol.

"Now!" Win shouted.

With Pugh and Chandler momentarily distracted by Dexter's action, Win and Joe were able to draw and fire. The night was lit by gun flashes. Pugh and Chandler, both of whom already had their weapons drawn, fired, but their missiles flew harmlessly into the dark, whereas both Win and Joe's bullets found their mark.

"No! No! Don't shoot! Don't shoot!" Coit shouted in fear, throwing his hands in the air. Jacoby, not willing to go against the Coulters alone, followed suit. Elam had no choice but to follow, because Dexter had picked up Elam's dropped pistol. The positions were now reversed. Those who had, but a heartbeat earlier, been the captors were now prisoners.

Chapter 22

THE SUN WAS FULL, FIRING THE MOUNTAINS WITH color and pushing back the chill. Win was sitting near the fire, drinking coffee. Joe was chewing on a piece of jerky. Looking sullen and a little frightened by the change in their fortunes, Coit, Jacoby, and Elam were sitting by the fire. Dexter was poking at the fire with a stick.

Sue was still asleep.

"I gotta piss," Jacoby said.

"So, piss."

"How'm I goin' to do that? My hands is tied."

Win started over toward him to untie his hands. As he did so, he saw something in Jacoby's pocket. "What's this?" he asked, reaching for it.

"That's mine," Jacoby said.

Win pulled it out. "I know this watch," he said. He remembered now. This was the watch Karen had worn on the dress she called her schoolmarm dress. "This belonged to Karen McKenzie. Joe told me she had been murdered, but I didn't think it had any connection to this. You killed her, didn't you?"

"What if I did?" Jacoby replied. "It's not like anyone

is going to cry over her. Hell, she wasn't nothin' but a whore. Killin' her was as easy as steppin' on a bug."

Win felt the anger boiling up inside. He drew back his hand to hit him, then turned and walked away to keep from hitting a man who couldn't hit back.

"Where you goin'? I told you I have to piss," Jacoby said again.

"Piss in your pants, you son of a bitch," Win growled.

"What do you plan to do with us?" Coit asked.

"I don't know. Turn you over to the law, I suppose."

Coit laughed. "What law? I'm a judge, Jacoby and Elam are law officers. Do you really think anyone would take your word against mine? Especially when I tell them you killed Mayor Pugh and Marshall Chandler as they were discharging their duty as officials of Goldslide."

"There is no town of Goldslide," Win said.

"Oh, but there is. As a circuit judge, I have the authority to issue a court order declaring the incorporation of a town and I have incorporated Goldslide."

Win looked at Dexter. "Is that right?"

"As ludicrous as it may seem, circuit judges do have the right to do that," Dexter said. He held his arm out. "Welcome to Goldslide, population, seven."

"There is a way out," Coit suggested. "Let us go, and I'll reverse my decision. I'll declare you innocent in the Taggert case. I'll also rule that you killed Pugh and Chandler in self-defense." Coit looked at Dexter. "I'll even reverse my decision on the rape case. I'll declare Taggert and Jacoby guilty."

"Hold it!" Jacoby said. "You're turnin' on your own friends?"

"Jacoby, disabuse yourself of any idea that you and I were ever friends," Coit said. "You are a pig of a man. You have been useful to me, but you have never been and could never be a friend."

"You know, Coit, I should've killed you a long time ago," Jacoby sneered.

"What about my offer?" Coit said to Win.

"We're supposed to do this and just all go on our way?" Win asked.

"Sure, why not?" Coit replied. "It turns out there's no gold here anyway. We have no reason to fight."

"Are we also to just forget about the innocent people who were murdered?" Dexter asked. "The assayer and the girl in Reveille?"

"I didn't kill them. Jacoby did," Coit said. "Besides, that has nothing to do with what is going on here."

Win stood up and walked away from the others. He looked out across the valley. The closest mountains were gold and silver in the morning sun. Each range beyond the first range progressed in color, from bright blue to deep purple. If such a place as Goldslide really did exist, its residents would have a beautiful view.

Suddenly Win smiled then turned and walked back to the fire. "We're going to have an election," he said.

"What?" Dexter asked.

"Mayor Pugh and Marshall Chandler are dead. The town of Goldslide needs new officers. Dexter, I nominate you as mayor, my brother as marshal, and myself as judge."

"What are you doing?" Coit asked. There was a frightened edge to his voice as he began to consider the possibilities.

"Are there any further nominations?"

Joe and Dexter stared at Win as if he had suddenly gone mad.

"No? Then all nominations are closed. Those who are in favor of the slate of candidates as presented, signify by raising your right hand." Win raised his hand, followed by Joe, and then, rather reluctantly, by Dexter. By now they realized that Win had something in mind, but they didn't know what.

"The slate of candidates has been duly elected." He turned to Coit. "Now, I can turn you in to the law," he said. "In fact, I'm turning you over to myself, because you, Jacoby, and Elam are going to be tried for murder in the court of Goldslide."

"What? Don't be ridiculous! You can't do that!" Coit said.

"Oh, but I can . . . and I will," Win said. "And, thanks to your court order . . . it will be legal."

"Wait a minute, Win, are you serious?" Dexter asked.

Win looked at the three prisoners. "I'm dead serious," he said. "We are going to try these three men right now, right here, in this newly incorporated town of Goldslide. And after we find them guilty, we are going to hang them from that cottonwood tree right over there."

Coit, Jacoby, and Elam blanched. In the morning light, their faces looked gray as mud-clay at a spring.

"You can't do this," Jacoby said. "You got no right to do this."

"Oh, but I do. Judge Coit provided the authority for me to do it. In fact, he was going to hold court himself, I believe."

"What about counsel?" Coit asked. "You can't have court without counsel."

"By a fortuitous set of circumstances, we have two lawyers here," Win said. By now Sue was awake, and, quietly, Dexter was filling her in on what was going on. "I intend to appoint one of them as your defense counsel and the other as prosecutor. You have your choice as to who you want."

"Some choice we have," Coit said, scoffing. "He nodded toward the two Davenports. Either a drunk or a female who hasn't yet passed the bar."

"That may be, but it is the only choice you have," Win said.

The three prisoners huddled together for a moment, then Coit spoke for them. "If there is no way out of this . . . then we choose Dexter Davenport to defend us."

"So ordered," Win said.

Dexter and Sue came over to speak to Win.

"You didn't ask us how we feel about this," Dexter said.

"How do you feel about it?"

"We don't want to do it."

"All right," Win said easily.

"That's it? You've changed your mind? You aren't going to have the trial?"

"Coit's right. We can't have a trial without lawyers, and you don't want to do it. So, I may as well shoot them," Win said. He started toward the prisoners, pulling his pistol as he did so.

"Wait!" Dexter called out to him.

Win paused and looked back at him.

"What are you going to do?"

"I told you, I'm going to shoot them," Win said easily.

"Just like that?"

"Just like that."

"How can you do such a thing?"

"Were you in the war, Dexter?"

"Uh, no," Dexter replied.

"I didn't think so. Let me tell you, Dexter, there were a lot of men killed during the war. In fact, I killed a lot of men during the war. Many of the men I killed . . . I would say that most of the men I killed . . . were good men. Family men, many of them, with a wife and kids at home. They were in the war fighting for what they believed in . . . just as I was. Now, I don't feel good about having killed those good men, Dexter, but it was war, and good men were killing good men on both sides."

Win pointed at the three prisoners. "Now, as far as I'm concerned, these men aren't good men. They are pond scum. Now, after all the good men I've killed, do

you think I would have a moment's hesitation in shooting men like these?"

Win raised his pistol and pointed it at Coit, then came
back on the hammer.

"Wait!" Dexter called. "We'll do it! We'll hold the
trial."

An eagle soared overhead with a struggling mouse in its
talons. Below that majestic bird's flight path, a strange
scene was taking place on the side of a mountain.

Six men and one woman, isolated from their fellow
creatures by many miles, dotted the landscape below in
a precise manner. Win was sitting authoritatively upon
a log. Sue stood just to one side of the log, while Joe
sat on a rock a few feet away. Coit, Jacoby, and Elam
stood with their hands tied behind them. Dexter con-
ferred earnestly with them.

"I now call this court to order," Win said. He nodded
toward Joe. "Joe will act as a juror. I will be both judge
and juror. We are convened to try Preston Coit, Moe
Jacoby, and Burt Elam on the charges of murder, conspiracy to commit murder, rape, misappropriation of a
mining claim, and robbery. How do you plead?"

"Your honor, defense moves that the charge of rape
be dropped from the indictment," Dexter said.

"Are you arguing that Jacoby did not rape your
daughter?" Win asked, surprised by Dexter's petition.

"I am not arguing that," Dexter said. "Whether he did
or did not rape Miss Davenport is irrelevant."

"How can it be irrelevant?"

"He has already been tried for that charge and found
not guilty. The principle of double jeopardy prohibits
him from being tried for the same charge a second time."

"All right, the charge of rape is dropped," Win said.
"How do the defendants plead to the remaining
charges?"

"They have refused to plea, Your Honor, so I will enter a plea for them. I plead not guilty."

"Mr. Davenport, you know damned well they are guilty," Win said in exasperation. "How can you plead them not guilty?"

"If they remain mute I have no choice but to plead not guilty on their behalf," Dexter replied. "If this court is to have any validity at all, then we must follow the law."

Win stroked his chin for a moment, then he nodded. "All right," he said. "Court accepts a plea of not guilty. Prosecution, you may begin."

"Your Honor," Dexter said again.

Win sighed. "What now, Mr. Davenport?"

"Your Honor, not only have the defendants refused to plead, but they have also refused to testify."

"No problem. I'll just order them to testify."

"You can't do that. No one can be forced to testify against themselves."

"Whose side are you on?" Win asked in exasperation.

"I'm an advocate for the defense, but I am on the side of the law," Dexter said. "What I'm saying is, since the defendants refuse to testify in their own behalf, we have no witnesses. With no witnesses, I see no need for opening statements. If there is no objection from the prosecution, I recommend that we go directly to summation."

"Do you object to that, Miss Davenport?" Win asked Sue.

"I have no objections, Your Honor."

"Very well, the court will hear summation. Mr. Davenport, you may begin. But, before you begin, let me tell you that you cannot make the argument that this court has no jurisdiction. You will make your summation exactly as if you were trying this case in any city in the country."

"Your Honor, under ordinary circumstances, I would petition the court to sever the case so that each defendant could stand trial on his own. Since these aren't ordinary circumstances, I will plead as if the cases are severed.

"I begin with the case against Burt Elam. I have personally known Elam for at least five years. I know him to be a man of less than average intelligence, who is mean-spirited and foul-mouthed. Such a person can be easily led by someone in authority, such as Preston Coit. Elam wears a badge, and Coit is a circuit judge. Therefore, Elam's very presence here is the result of his genuine belief that he is acting in the line of the duty of his office.

"Low intelligence, mean spirit, a foul mouth, and acquiescence to authority are not, of themselves, violations of the law. I have never witnessed Elam commit murder, conspire to commit murder, nor indeed, break the law in any way. And I am certain this court will be unable to produce a witness who will testify otherwise. I therefore suggest that Burt Elam be found totally innocent of all charges.

"With regard to Moe Jacoby, I plead not guilty."

"How can you plead him not guilty?" Win demanded. He pointed to Jacoby. "He confessed to killing Alice McKenzie."

"Your Honor, please. Allow me to conduct my case," Dexter said.

"Yeah, all right. Go ahead," Win said.

"Jacoby is not guilty by reason of insanity. You are correct, Your Honor, when you say that, with our own ears, we heard Jacoby admit to murdering Alice McKenzie. We also heard him say that killing her was no more traumatic for him than stepping on a bug.

"I submit to you that no one can kill as easily as stepping on a bug, unless it is the result of an aberrant mental condition. Another word for aberrant mental behavior is insane. And, in our legal system, someone who is insane—even criminally insane—cannot be held accountable for their actions. Moe Jacoby is obviously insane and, therefore, not guilty.

"And, finally, we come to Judge Preston Coit. Judge Coit is, admittedly, the most difficult of the three to put a handle on. He is a brilliant and learned man, who, for some time, has occupied a position of power and prestige. Such men sometimes step outside society's boundaries, simply because the temptation to do so is matched by the power to do so.

"There is no doubt that Judge Coit is such a man. However, we are convened to try him, not for malfeasance in office, but for murder and conspiracy to commit murder. And, whereas we have validation from Jacoby's own lips that he committed murder, we have no such confession from Judge Coit. I submit, therefore, that without compelling evidence, eyewitnesses who can testify to fact, or his confession, we have no choice but to find Preston Coit not guilty.

"Defense rests."

Chapter 23

ALTHOUGH DEXTER DAVENPORT WAS DEFENDING THE man who had raped her, as well as the man who had given the rapist a pass in that mockery of a trial two years earlier, Sue Davenport was never more proud of her father than she was at that very moment. There, on the side of a mountain, in a raw and lawless land, she had seen law practiced by a man of principle and dignity.

"Is prosecution ready for summation?" Win asked.

"I am," Sue said.

"I hope you are," Win said. "Because the truth is, your father has put up a powerful defense for the indefensible."

Sue looked over at her father and at the three defendants. "He has, hasn't he?" she said proudly.

"Make your case, girl," Win said, not as a judge, but as a man who truly wanted to see justice done.

"Your Honor, the defense made an effort to sever the case in his presentation. It is his contention that Burt Elam is not guilty by reason of low intelligence and lack of self esteem . . . that Moe Jacoby is innocent by reason of insanity . . . and that Preston Coit is not guilty because of the lack of any factual witnesses or a confession.

"But I would argue that the case cannot be severed. We cannot plead their cases individually, because while we are dealing with more than one person, we are also dealing with the unifying charge of conspiracy. A conspiracy is a whole, and once something becomes whole, it can never again be separated. Apple pie consists of apples, sugar, flour, cinnamon, and butter. Those are all individual things, but once they are assembled and baked, they become a pie, and no matter how small a piece you cut . . . you always have apple pie.

"That being the case, Your Honor, the guilt of one of these defendants is the guilt of all of them. Therefore, as the prosecutor, I am going to focus on the one for whom we do have hard evidence, in the form of a watch that he stole from the body of his victim. We also have a confession.

"By his own words, Jacoby is guilty of murder. We don't know how many more murders he has committed, but we do know that he attempted to murder Win and Joe Coulter.

"Defense has suggested that Jacoby might be insane, for no sane person, he says, could kill someone as easily as stepping on a bug. But I say we must disallow the plea of insanity, in order to find this man, and these men, guilty as charged. But how can we find him sane? For what sane man could commit crimes with such lack of passion?

"The answer is . . . no man could, if we gauge sanity by the standards of moral men. But this man . . . these men . . . are not moral. Therefore the only test of sanity we need to hold up to the light is whether he was a man of reason when he committed the crime. Was Moe Jacoby a man of reason?

"I call your attention to the fact that he held a gun to my head. He then announced in a loud voice that he would shoot me . . . and my father. His *reason* for that was to force you, Your Honor, and you, Mr. Juror, to come in from the dark with your hands in the air. He was therefore aware that the threat to kill me was something that would disturb you. He could not reason such a thing unless he had the tool of reason in the grasp of his mind. He could not threaten if he was not aware that killing was an evil thing.

"Therefore, Your Honor, I submit that Moe Jacoby is fully in possession of reason and is aware of right from wrong. That awareness of right and wrong is all that is required for him to be legally sane.

"If you accept this logic, then you must declare him sane, and if he is sane, then he stands convicted, and condemned by his own words.

"If justice is truly to be served in this court of ours, if the truth will come out here on this lonely mountainside in the midst of some of the most beautiful country God ever created, then there can be only one verdict rendered, and that verdict is guilty. And, because they are part of a conspiracy—part of a whole—the guilt of Moe Jacoby, is the guilt of them all.

"The prosecution rests."

"Court will recess while the jury decides," Win said. Nodding at his brother, he got up from the log and the two of them walked away for a little distance to discuss the verdict.

"What do you think?" Joe asked.

"The girl was good, wasn't she?" Win asked.

"Yes, she was. But so was the father," Joe replied.

"Yeah. Especially his argument about Elam. I think he's right. I think Elam is just an ignorant shit that got caught up in this. He was too damn dumb to get out of it."

"What about the girl saying you can't separate them?" Joe asked.

"She made a good point, I agree. But I figure this is a hanging case, and like Dexter said, a fella ought not

to be hung just because he's dumb. I say we find Coit
and Jacoby guilty, and we cut Elam loose."

"All right," Joe agreed.

Returning, Win called the court back to order.

"It is the decision of this court that the defendant, Burt
Elam, be found not guilty."

"What?" Elam said, a broad smile on his face.
"You're findin' me not guilty?"

"Untie him, Joe."

Joe untied Elam and Elam began immediately to rub
his wrists.

"Step away from the other prisoners please," Win
said.

"Yes, sir!" Elam said. He started toward his gun, then
stopped and looked up at Win. "Is it all right if I pick
up my gun?"

"Yes," Win said. "But keep it in your holster."

"What about us?" Coit said.

"The court finds Preston Coit and Moe Jacoby guilty
and sentences you both to hang. Sentence to be carried
out immediately. Elam, help my brother get these two
mounted."

"Yes, sir," Elam said, as subservient now to Win as
he had been to Coit before.

"No!" Coit shouted. "No, you can't do this!"

"I can and I will," Win said.

Protesting every inch of the way, the two men were
set on horseback and moved into position under the tree.
Joe and Elam threw ropes over the limb, then tied and
looped nooses around the necks of the condemned men.
All was ready.

"Have you men any last words?" Win asked, looking
up at them. He stood on the ground nearby with his feet
set wide apart.

Coit shut his eyes and shook his head, but said nothing.

"Yeah," Jacoby said. "Yeah, I got me somethin' to

say." He looked at Sue Davenport. "Come over here honey," he said. "Open up your shirt and show me your titties while my neck's bein' stretched. That way I'll have somethin' to tell ole Taggert when I run into him down in hell." Jacoby began to laugh.

"Carry out the sentence," Win said to Joe, but before Joe could do so, Dexter, with a yell of rage, startled both horses and they leaped forward. The ropes pulled the men out of the saddles, choking Jacoby's laughter off into a death rattle.

It was deathly quiet, save for a creaking sound as the two men turned slowly at the end of the ropes. It had been nearly five minutes since the horses bolted, almost four minutes since the last twitch from either of the bodies.

"Cut them down," Win ordered.

Joe and Elam cut the men down and laid them out under the tree. Win looked over at Sue and saw a pinched, uncertain expression on her face.

"Are you all right?" he asked.

"I don't know. I've never done murder before," she said in a small voice.

"This wasn't murder. This was an execution."

"But . . . was it legal?" Sue asked.

"Yes," Dexter said resolutely.

"Pa, do you really think so?"

Dexter nodded. "I must confess that I had some reservations about it at first, but I now believe it was legal," Dexter said. "We are legally constituted as a town, and as such, are empowered to elect officials, including a judge. In the past several years there have been scores, perhaps hundreds of hangings in the West, with no more validity than we have. And those that have been looked into by higher courts have, for the most part, been upheld. It's a brutal business, but we live in a brutal world." He looked at Coit's body. "Poor Coit. By making Goldslide a legal entity, he was the instrument of his own destruction."

"Yeah," Elam said. He giggled, madly. "I reckon he's already holdin' court down there in hell."

"Elam," Win said.

"Yes, sir?" Elam replied.

"Have you ever been to California?"

Elam shook his head. "California? No, I never been there."

"Go."

"I beg your pardon?"

"Get on your horse and go to California," Win said.

"I ain't got nothin' to see in California. Besides, I'm the sheriff of Horseshoe."

Win shook his head. "Not anymore," he said. "And if I ever see you in Horseshoe again . . . in fact, if I ever see you anywhere in Nevada again, I'll kill you."

"But . . . you said I was innocent."

"This has nothing to do with guilt or innocence. This has to do with I don't like you." Win took Karen's watch from his pocket and looked at it. "If I were you, I'd start now," he said. "If you are still within rifle range two minutes from now, I'll shoot you. Do you understand that?"

Elam didn't even try to answer. Instead he ran to his horse, leaped into the saddle, then, slapping his legs against the animal's side, rode away at a gallop. As he rode, he was chased down the mountainside by the laughter of the last four residents of the town of Goldslide.

JAKE LOGAN
TODAY'S HOTTEST ACTION WESTERN!